DUBAI
TALES

by

Muhammad al Murr

FOREST
BOOKS
London & Boston

Translated by
Peter Clark

PUBLISHED BY
FOREST BOOKS

20 Forest View, Chingford, London E4 7AY, UK
16 Lincoln Road, Wayland, MA 01778, USA

FIRST PUBLISHED 1991

Typeset in Great Britain by Cover to Cover, Cambridge
Printed in Great Britain by BPCC Wheatons Ltd, Exeter

British Library Cataloguing in Publication Data:
Al Murr, Muhammad
Dubai tales.
I. Title
892.736 [F]

Library of Congress Catalogue Card No:
90–71091

ISBN 0 948259 86 8

Contents

Bibliographical Note

'Father and Son' is translated from a story, first published in the collection, *Hubb min Nau' Akhar*, Dar al Auda, Beirut, 1982.

'Antar', 'Your Uncle was a Poet', 'One Day a Week', 'Six Letters' and 'Problem and Solution' are from *Sadaqa*, Dar al Auda, Beirut, 1984.

'An Icy Marriage' is from *Al Mufaja'a*, Dar al Auda, Beirut, 1985.

'Pepsi' is from *Shai' min al Hanan*, Al Bayan Trading Press, Dubai, 1985.

'A Small Ad in the Newspaper' and 'A One-off Encounter' are from *Nasib*, Dar al Auda, Beirut, 1986.

'Jasmine' and 'Look After Yourself' are from *Yasmin*, Dar al Auda, Beirut, 1986.

'Bombay or Bust', 'A Late Dinner' and 'Study Course' are from *Makan fi'l Qalb*, Al Bayan Trading Press, Dubai, 1988.

'Pleasures of the Night' is from *Habuba*, Dar al Auda, Beirut, 1988.

'In the Mortuary' and 'The Long Awaited Trip' are from *Qurrat al'Ain*, Al Bayan Trading Press, Dubai, 1988.

'The Light that Shines no More', 'Influence' and 'Fear' are from *Al Sawt al Na'im*, Al Bayan Trading Press, Dubai, 1989.

Introduction

M uhammad al Murr was born in Dubai in 1955 and studied at Syracuse University in the United States. He has worked as a journalist and is the best-known writer of the United Arab Emirates.

Between 1982 and 1989 he published eleven collections of short stories. Of the 144 stories that have appeared in these volumes I have selected twenty one. The selection has been based on a number of criteria. The most significant has been that I liked them. I have also tried to present the range and development of Muhammad al Murr as a writer. I have chosen some stories that he has particularly liked. I have also been guided by the preferences of others.

All illustrate vividly aspects of the lives and values of the people of Dubai. For a century and more Dubai has been a major trading port in the Gulf with strong links with the countries further to the east. Since the 1960s — within Muhammad al Murr's own lifetime — the oil wealth of the region combined with the commercial skill of the people have transformed Dubai into a prosperous city. The expectations of the people of Dubai have expanded but traditional values based on Islam and family solidarity have survived and adjusted to a new world.

This is the social background to Muhammad al Murr's stories which are occasionally nostalgic, sometimes funny but always humane and unfailingly perceptive.

In preparing this collection I am grateful for their comments and suggestions to Theresa Alleguen Clark, Rebecca Bradley, Jack Briggs, Marie-Reine Shehayed and, not least, the author himself.

Peter Clark, *Abu Dhabi*, 1990

Muhammad al Murr

Muhammad al Murr was born in Dubai in 1955. He is a graduate of Syracuse University in the United States and has worked as a journalist in Dubai. He has published eleven volumes of short stories and one book on the popular language of the Gulf.

Peter Clark

Peter Clark was born in 1939. He is the author of *Marmaduke Pickthall, British Muslim* and translated *Karari: the Sudanese Account of the Battle of Omdurman* by Ismat Hasan Zulfo. He has worked for the British Council since 1967.

1

A Study Course

I

This was the first time that Khawla's husband, Abdul Aziz, would be going away since they got married nine months earlier. She sorted out his clothes and other requirements to put in the big suitcase he would take with him. She packed overcoats, shirts, jeans, a radio and cassette player and some tapes. He was shaving in the bathroom. She called out to him and asked, 'How many bars of soap do you want me to pack for you?'

He laughed and said, 'Why are you packing soap? Am I going to a remote village or to some tiny mountain town? I'm going to London, capital city for the manufacture of soap and of everything else.'

Khawla smiled and said, 'I don't want you to be short of anything.'

Abdul Aziz came out of the bathroom, drying his face, and hugged her.

'Don't worry', he said.

She said affectionately, 'Promise me you'll write every day.'

'It's old fashioned to write letters,' he smiled. 'You know that at school I got the lowest marks in composition. The Arabic teacher used to tell me in front of the class that when he read something I'd written he felt that Ibn al Muqaffa and Jahiz and Manfaluti would be turning over in their graves in horror. Today telephone calls are less hassle and more personal.'

II

The next day Khawla had the first telephone conversation with her husband. He told her that the journey was exhausting and that they were delayed for six hours at Amsterdam airport because of poor weather conditions. An Englishman sitting next to him had too much to drink and was sick over his food tray. The weather in London was cold and wet. The flat provided by the Institute was very small and in an old building, and he was thinking of renting a bigger place in Edgware Road with a lot more comforts, like a large refrigerator, a colour television and video, armchairs and a comfortable bed. He told his wife playfully that he had read in an English newspaper about a Moroccan woman who had given birth to five babies. He hoped she would be pregnant with five babies one day. She could then retire from pregnancy and having babies.

III

During the first week, Abdul Aziz got to know all the other students on the management course. He chatted and joked with them during and between lectures. On the third day of the course he announced that it was his birthday and invited them all to a dinner party to celebrate that happy event at one of the Arab restaurants in Queensway. He took great pains ordering for his guests many different kinds of *hors d'oeuvres*, main courses, sweets and drinks. After that auspicious party Abdul Aziz became the undoubted star of the course and the most popular person among both students and the English staff who had been filled with mazza and Lebanese arak. Abdul Aziz was pleased with the attention given by his colleagues and teachers and especially by the interest shown by one French student, Christine. She was thirty years old, four years older than he was. But she seemed to be only twenty, or so it seemed to Abdul Aziz who always used to say that European women looked after themselves as far as food and physical exercise were concerned. They never appeared flabby and never had any of the symptoms of premature old age – weariness or lethargy or excessive fatness.

2

Abdul Aziz returned Christine's interest. He told her that he loved France and thought Paris was the most beautiful city in the world. French food was the best and tastiest food that existed. He told her that his favourite novel was *Les Misérables* by Victor Hugo and that he had wept tears of bitterness at the sad ending of the book. He wished French had been the set language for students in his country from the first grade of primary school to the last year at university. Christine had no need of all this adulation for France and the French. She was imbued with a *joie de vivre* that allowed her to enjoy the pleasures of life to the full, easily and openly, free from restraint or inhibition.

At the end of the first week Abdul Aziz took Christine to a restaurant at the Hilton Hotel where they had an alcoholic cocktail mixed with orange squash, coconut and tomato. After dinner they went to the hotel ballroom and spent the night in riotous pleasure.

Abdul Aziz was woken next morning by the constant ringing of the telephone. When he tried to get out of bed he stumbled over the sleeping body of Christine beside him. He went round the bed and took up the receiver. Khawla's voice came through, scolding him.

'Why didn't you get in touch with me and give me the telephone number at your new flat? I got it from your mother.'

'I was intending to contact you this morning because at the weekend I can talk a long time. I miss you.'

She said, with a pretence of anger, 'Miss me? Are you already fed up with English girls?'

He looked at Christine, who was still asleep.

'English girls! God help me! I swear to you in the name of my dear mother and on your darling head that I detest and abhor English girls.'

'Strange. Why so?'

'Because they are skinny and have long noses.'

He remembered that his wife was slim and that her nose was on the long side. He corrected himself.

'And above all else they are filthy dirty. They only have a shower once every ten days or once a month.'

'How have you got to know all that?'

Another problem. How could he extricate himself from that predicament? He quickly found his way out and said, 'Your brother, Abdullah, told me. You know he spent three years in Britain.'

Khawla changed the subject. 'Has the weather got any better?'
'It's still very cold and there's rain almost every day.'
'What are you doing today?'
'I'm going to stay in the flat. I've got a lot of work to go over and the weather isn't encouraging.'

Christine woke up and went to the bathroom. Abdul Aziz went on, 'I've put your picture on the desk where I do my research and read my reports.'

Her photograph was still at the bottom of the suitcase with some jallabiyas and vests.

'Your picture is the only thing that's getting me through this frightful separation.'

Christine came out of the bathroom with a large white towel wrapped round her. She looked like a beautiful chubby goose. Abdul Aziz smiled at her and carried on talking to his wife.

'All the English girls aren't worth your little finger nail.'

His wife felt pleased and asked him, 'Are you happy with the food?'

'There's nothing wrong with the food, but there are plenty of Arab and Indian restaurants. But my palate enjoys only the food cooked by your beloved hands. Even the cheese and tomato sandwiches you prepare quickly when you don't want to cook a full meal are to me more tasty than the finest food I could eat in London restaurants.'

He asked after her mother, her brother and his family. And that concluded the conversation. Christine meanwhile had prepared a light breakfast of fried eggs, cheese and olives. Abdul Aziz theatrically breathed in the smell of fried eggs.

'How superb is the smell of eggs fried by your beautiful hands! Your fine French taste makes even this humble breakfast seem like a magnificent banquet.'

They sat eating and planning how to spend the sunny day – a walk in Hyde Park, lunch at an Arab restaurant in Edgware Road, the new James Bond film, and finally dinner at a French restaurant in Piccadilly.

IV

In the second week Khawla's friend, Samia, invited her to spend Thursday and Friday at the family farm near Dhaid. The December air was refreshing and gentle. Khawla had been bored and jumped at the idea. Samia's brother, Khalid, drove from Dubai to Dhaid. The car was filled with girls, for in addition to Samia and Khawla, there were his two other sisters, Aisha and Ulya, his aunt and her two daughters. Before her marriage, Khawla used to enjoy Khalid's company and to delight in his conversation. During the journey Khalid, by word and gesture, flirted with Khawla. His sisters and aunt took no specific notice of his conversation, with its smartness, its charm and the way it inserted significant private allusions into general conversation. He mentioned some poem and Khawla knew that he was referring to her. He spoke of some films and plays, praising actresses who resembled her in height, build, facial structure, length of hair and colour of eyes. He praised the colour green and said that doctors reckoned that colour calmed the nerves. She was wearing a green dress.

All that evening and the following morning when they went to the beaches at Khor Fukkan and Dibba the private conversation, the allusive remarks, the secret praise, the gestures, the glances and the smiles between Khawla and Khalid combined to produce the effect of magic. When they were on the way home on Friday evening and the sun was setting on the sand hills of Dhaid, giving the horizon an extraordinary colour, the sentimental reunion and mutual attraction were perfect.

At ten that night Khawla's telephone rang. She knew that it was Khalid. They talked about the beauty of nature and the outing they had just returned from. They discussed the many problems of contemporary life, and the absence of friendship in this materialist world, where people were only concerned about themselves. Wives no longer felt at home with their husbands, sons were no longer at ease with fathers, mothers and daughters no longer understood each other. They agreed to meet alone so they could better understand each other, and talk about the friendship that nobody appreciated these days. When Khawla came home after the first rendezvous alone with Khalid, she felt very happy. It was humid and she took a quick shower. The telephone rang. She put on a bathrobe, came out of the bathroom, picked up the receiver. It was her husband. She was a bit disappointed at first but soon recovered her liveliness and spontaneity.

Abdul Aziz asked with some irritation, 'I tried to contact you three times. Where were you?'

5

'I was in the garden seeing to the lovely roses that your dear hands planted three months ago. The blooms are more beautiful than the one on the seed packet.'

Abdul Aziz felt reassured.

'And how is the cat, Nunu? Is she sitting by the TV as usual?'

Khawla said lovingly, 'Nunu misses you. Since you went away her eyes have been glued to the door waiting for you to come back.'

'Have you been out with your friends shopping, or on outings?'

Khawla replied sadly, 'Very occasionally, and even then I'm conscious that you are not with me. I feel like a poor orphan girl. When I go with friends to places you and I used to go to, I feel heartbroken and almost cry.'

Abdul Aziz sympathised with what his wife was saying.

'And I, my darling, I feel that this noisy big city with all its variety without you, is just a huge cemetery crushed by silence and over which hover gloom and despondency.'

'Without you this house is a museum of sad memories', Khawla said tearfully. 'Even the air I breathe alone is stifling, the water I drink and the food I eat have no savour when you're not with me. All the pleasures and joys of life that soothe the spirit whenever you are around are turned to dust and ashes. My lonely, weary heart is burdened with care.'

V

Abdul Aziz went on seeing Christine and deepened his love affair with France, French food and culture, especially when Christine talked about her country cottage overlooking the sea in the northern province of Brittany. And Khawla continued her discussions with Khalid both by telephone and also during meetings alone with him. They talked basically about friendship and the very special relationship they had and the need to keep it away from the eyes, ears and tongues of people who did not understand or appreciate the meaning of true friendship, but only considered the material and sensual aspects. These, they agreed, were minor when compared with the profound and more deeply emotional aspects.

The telephone conversations between Abdul Aziz and Khawla also went on without interruption. They vied with each other in complaining of the anguish of their separation and the torment of loneliness. As the end of the course approached, so the complaints increased, the moans got louder and sobbing and tears became more and more frequent.

VI

The married couple met at Dubai airport. Their chauffeur slowly drove their car away from the numerous taxis lined up outside the arrival hall. They held hands and wept tears of happiness at the reunion.

'This is the last time you go on a study course', Khawla said.

He smiled, as he recalled Christine's powerful scent.

'Don't feel too upset by it all. You know that study courses are very important for my career.'

She recalled Khalid's whispers and dreamy eyes, 'I'm sorry, my love. Yes, your future is our future and your success is our success.'

2
Six Letters

I

Bombay, 1 October 1970

To my dear brother, Abdullah Khalifa,
Greetings,

We reached Bombay a week ago. Uncle Salim was longing to see the city as if he was coming here as a tourist rather than for medical treatment. I knew that his illness was serious but they would not tell us anything about it in the hospitals in Dubai. Indeed we were advised to take him abroad for treatment. We went first to the Orient Hotel near the fruit and vegetable market. The rates were reasonable but the hotel was filthy: there were rats running about the room bigger than cats. After a couple of days we transferred to the Apollo Hotel in the Coloba district. It costs a little more, the daily rate being thirty rupees, but the hotel is clean. We were taken there by Ahmad Khalfan, the only person from Dubai who lives in that hotel. Most people stay in the Travellers' Rest House, the Orient, the Metropole or the Suna Mahal.

Ahmad Khalfan is a decent chap and helped us persuade Uncle Salim to go into hospital for some tests and after that helped us get him into the Bombay hospital. He knows most of the doctors there because he has had a number of operations in the place – hernia, piles, ulcers, appendicitis – and he is always telling us about these

9

operations with detailed enthusiasm. How he went into hospital and joked with the nurses, his friendship with the doctors, how they put him under anaesthetic, how he felt when he recovered from the anaesthetic and found himself in a public ward with other patients, how after the operation they showed him the piece of his body that had been cut off. You would imagine when you listen to that man as he talks about the operations he has had that surgical operations were more like a picnic outing full of fun and nothing to do with pain or discomfort.

At the hospital they have carried out a lot of tests and analyses. They have told us that the results would be available in three days time and we are now waiting for them. Yesterday I saw Khalfan bin Atiq, one of the senior customs officials, at the hospital. That great giant of a man who used to be the terror of every captain, boatman and official, has been reduced to a shadow of his former self. He has become very thin and his voice is faint. He has even become shorter. He greeted me cheerfully and started to chat, asking for news from Dubai. Heaven's above, who would have said that Khalfan bin Atiq would become so unassertive? They say he has TB. He no longer dyes his white hair. Even his eyelashes and eyebrows are white. The husband of his only daughter was with him. This chap never knew how to smile. I reckon in his heart of hearts he wants Khalfan to die so his wife can inherit all the money he has gathered together by one means or another.

The things I brought with me – the recorder, the radio and the two watches – I have sold at cost price, so I have not made a single rupee. I think the dealer must have cheated me: better luck next time. I did not come to India on business, but to accompany Uncle Salim. I do hope God restores his health to him.

My greetings to your good self and to all the family and friends and to anybody who asks after us.

Ever yours sincerely,

Your brother, Muhammad Khalifa.

II

Bombay, 8 October 1970

To my dear brother, Abdullah Khalifa,
Greetings,

My worst expectations have been realised. They told us at the hospital that Uncle Salim has skin cancer and that he must be under regular medical observation and treatment for the next four months. When we went back to the hotel that morning I tried to lighten the impact of the news for him. I told him of the great mercy of God, Who was full of kindness towards those who worshipped Him and that recovery was in His hands. Many patients for whom people had given up hope had been restored to health, getting the better of the disease and their trials. In the taxi and all the time at the hotel he muttered not a single word. His face was rigid as if he did not hear what I was saying. I had no idea what was going on in his mind, whether it was terror of death or hopes of getting better. After evening prayers he looked at me while he was still kneeling on the prayer rug, and said in a voice full of sadness and despair, 'How is it that I have cancer? I feel no great pain in my body. It seems that nowadays death takes people very calmly and without any discomfort.'

He left the hotel after that and I went out with him. He started to wander around the Gateway of India and to look at the ocean waves. For four hours we walked along the road that overlooks the sea. I tried to talk but he silenced me with one glance of fury. Near the Gateway of India he saw three Indian musicians, one beating a drum, a second on an ancient fiddle that was falling to pieces and the third on a local musical instrument like the accordion. They were just playing, not singing. After a while we realised that all three were dumb and had lost any capacity to talk or to sing. Uncle Salim gave them ten rupees. They were overjoyed. We sat down by them and they played joyous music, sad music, strange music. They proposed that we join them in smoking hashish but we said no. We stayed with them until sunset when we went back to the hotel. My spirits full of gloom, it was a pain to watch Uncle Salim drag his feet one after the other. After a rest and dinner I wanted to cheer him up and so took him to Chowpatty Beach. He strolled along the beach dejectedly as if he was walking in the funeral procession of a dear lost friend.

He looked at a group of beggars – lepers and deformed people – and said, 'These people are luckier than I am with all their deformities. They are breathing the air of life and gathering money, eating and shitting and sleeping, knowing that they will wake up alive. If they do not have their own family, at least members of the human race treat them with charity whenever they take pity on them and toss them a few coins.' Then he pointed up to some seagulls and crows gathering on the beach. He said, 'These birds are more fortunate than I am. Even the turtles and fish in the sea are luckier than me. They fly and swim. They live.' A young man rode by on a white horse. The horse nearly knocked us down. I pulled Uncle Salim out of its path. He said with mordant bitterness, 'When I was a lad I was wilder and stronger than that horse.'

We came across a group of people in a circle which opened up as we went by. .We entered the circle and saw an Indian who had buried himself in the sand vertically. Only his head remained above the ground. Around his head had been drawn five circles coloured red, yellow and green. People were tossing coins into those circles. When Uncle Salim saw the sight of that man's head and face smiling as people were throwing more and more money he laughed sadly and observed, 'I'm like that Indian with only a head left. The illness has buried me and in a few days it will cover my head as well.'

I did my best to cheer him up but it was useless. Since that day he has only left the hotel to go to the hospital. The only good thing in his situation is that he is punctilious in taking the injections and swallowing the medicine in spite of constantly expressed doubts about their efficacy.

I would beg of you not to tell his wife and daughters about the matter of cancer. Tell them he has ulcers and piles or some less serious disease. We do not want to alarm them before it is necessary. I pray to God that he gets better.

My greetings to your dear self and to all the family and friends, to each and every dear one of you.

Sincerely your brother, Muhammad Khalifa.

III

Bombay, 20 October 1970

To my dear brother, Abdullah Khalifa,
Greetings,

We have received the letter you sent by the hand of Ali al Nashi who arrived in Bombay two days ago. It gives us comforting news of yourselves, family and friends. Khalfan bin Atiq died two days ago and for the first time I saw his son-in-law smiling as he gave me the news in the Padishah refreshment bar. When Uncle Salim heard the news his spirits went from bad to worse. He started going out of the hotel without informing me. I would go out looking for him, asking after him. Sometimes I found him weeping in a mosque and at other times I would bring him back in the small hours from a brothel in Faris Road. He would repeat all the time, 'I've been unlucky all my life. When I was small I was the pupil the teacher beat more than anybody else. As a result of the beatings I never learnt a thing. All my friends became merchants. They sold sugar, smuggled in gold, bought wine and contraband hashish and made thousands and thousands. I had no such luck and remained an obscure grocer. Even the woman I married wasn't pretty. She produced only daughters and now I'm dying, ill in a foreign country.'
He is still meticulous in having his injections and taking his pills. He asked me to write to you to say he wanted you to send 50,000 rupees. I do not know why he wants that huge sum. Perhaps he wishes to perform a deed of charity for the poor of whom there are so many in this city. On Sunday I took him to the races. When the horse on which he had placed a bet won, I saw the first smile on his face for many days.
I have frequently asked the doctor treating him about his condition. He brushes me off, saying, 'If he required an operation, the doctors could perform one on him without any bother, but it is a strange disease.'
My greetings to your dear self and to all the family and friends. Ever yours sincerely,

Your brother, Muhammad Khalifa.

IV

Bombay, 10 November 1970

To my dear brother, Abdullah Khalifa,
Greetings,

The money order you sent has arrived. Uncle Salim started spending it in an extraordinary way. He has insisted on getting married. I tried to stop him but was quite unable to do so. From what Ali al Nashi says, the Indian girl he has married has already been married four times. She married three men from Dubai one after the other and one man from Sharjah. I warned Uncle Salim about this but he took no notice and went ahead with his marriage plans. On the wedding night after all the arrangements had been finalised we brought the bride to the hotel. Uncle Salim gave the taxi driver thirty rupees and the hotel servants, each one, ten rupees. The next day he went with his bride to Bhendi Bazaar and bought her a taxi load of perfumes and clothes.

Yesterday he insisted on another whim. He wanted to construct a boat in the city of Calicut in the Malabar area. He was persuaded to do this by a boat captain who constructs boats in Calicut and then sails them to the ports of the Gulf. He told Uncle that the expenses of building a boat in Malabar are one third of the expenses of building a boat in any of the ports of the Gulf. Uncle Salim told me that this boat would, after his death, provide for his wife and daughters an income that would safeguard them from dire need and from the shame of having to beg. I tried in vain to divert him from his resolution. Tomorrow we – Uncle Salim, his wife and I – take the train for Calicut so he can supervise the start of the boat building. The doctor has given us the pills and the necessary syringes to take with us for the journey. When I get back I will write to you about the developments that will have taken place.

My greetings to your deaf self and to all the family and to friends and to all who ask after us.

Ever yours sincerely,

Your brother, Muhammad Khalifa.

V

Bombay, 1 December 1970

To my dear brother, Abdullah Khalifa,
Greetings,

We have come back to Bombay after Uncle Salim bought his boat for 40,000 rupees in Calicut. It is at the moment being repaired. The doctor has not told us whether he is any better or whether the disease has developed. He tells us that they will continue to treat him. The only thing that is satisfactory is that he is still extremely conscientious about taking his medicine. He is also shedding his gloomy thoughts and is beginning to assert himself. This shows up in what he says and in his face which is now radiant with smiles if not with laughter, especially when he jokes with his Indian wife. He has also disclosed to us that she had been married to two other Arabs in addition to the four we were told about by Ali al Nashi: one from Bahrain and one from Ajman. This fresh disclosure has had absolutely no effect on Uncle Salim's attitude towards his new wife: he has recently bought her four new gold bracelets.

It is very cold these days and there are continuous storms coming from the sea. In spite of this Uncle Salim goes for long walks with his Indian wife each day near the Gateway of India and on the road overlooking the turbulent ocean. He wears only his white thawb and red head dress.

Yesterday I saw at the Aisha hospital Ali al Nashi's sister. They have brought her here for an operation in her ear. Do you remember when she got married? I nearly died of grief over it all. It is strange how people change. When I saw her in the hospital with her fat cheeks and wild stare I was amazed that once upon a time I used to consider her the most beautiful woman in the world.

My greetings to your dear self and to all the family and to friends.

Ever yours sincerely,

Your brother, Muhammad Khalifa.

VI

Bombay, 1 January 1971

To my dear brother, Abdullah Khalifa,
Greetings,

Our trials are now over. The senior doctor at the hospital has told us that Uncle Salim has successfully completed his course of treatment and has triumphed over the disease. There are some pills and injections needed to complete the treatment. Uncle Salim will be able to take them under the supervision of a Dubai hospital.

We are now getting ready to come back to Dubai. Uncle Salim has divorced his Indian wife. She was most upset at first but calmed down and was quite satisfied when after the divorce he bought her ten new gold bracelets and a taxi load of silk cloth. He is now negotiating to sell the boat he bought to one of the captains even though he may incur a loss of two or three thousand rupees. With what is left he is buying some cloth and some perfume for his daughters and their mother. In a week's time we shall be with you in Dubai.

My greetings to your dear self and to all our family and to friends and to any who ask after us.

Ever yours sincerely,

Your brother, Muhammad Khalifa.

3
Pepsi

Abdulla came in through the door from the courtyard and his wife who was standing outside the kitchen dropped the radio she was carrying. Her husband smiled. His wife was astonished at the sight of the animal he was leading by a rope.

'What's that?' she shouted in amazement.

He smiled. 'Don't you know what this is?'

'I know what it is,' she answered in the same tone. 'But whose is it and why have you brought it here?'

The young camel turned its head to the right and to the left inspecting the courtyard.

'Uncle Khalifa gave it to us for Rashid. Its mother has died. He's got lots of camels to look after and doesn't want to be bothered with this one.'

At that moment the boy Rashid came out of his room and went into the courtyard where his parents stood by the young camel. Abdulla handed the rope that held the young camel over to his son who took it hesitantly. His mother then snatched the rope from him and returned it brusquely to her husband.

'My boy does not want some troublesome beast,' she said.

Her husband was taken aback.

'Whoever said that this young camel is a troublesome beast?'

'All camels are troublesome beasts. And wild. Don't you re-member the camel that bit your uncle's arm? It bit it off.'

When Rashid heard these words he fled behind his mother.

'That was thirty years ago,' Abdulla laughed. 'The camel was upset because my uncle used to beat it every day. He did it from self-defence.'

'That doesn't matter. My boy does not want this stupid animal.'

The young camel leant down and picked up in its mouth one of the wife's thawbs that was lying on the ground. The wife saw it and kicked the camel's head.

'Look,' she shouted. 'Right now it's wanting to eat us.'

'He's hungry,' her husband smiled. 'Give him some milk.'

'I'll give him poison,' she shouted angrily.

'What's all this fuss about?' her husband cried.

'I'm not going to feed this wild creature,' she shouted back. 'It'll eat my boy.'

The shouting and screaming and accusations got louder. The young camel was behind Abdulla and Rashid shrank behind his mother. The issue was not resolved in the mother's interest. She took the boy into the bedroom and Abdulla took the camel to one side of the courtyard where he tied him up.

During the forty days the young camel stayed in Abdulla's house, his wife refused to feed it, to water it or to pay it any attention whatsoever. She would not let her son go anywhere near it. Her husband's pleadings and threats were of no use in making her change her mind. He had to do everything himself. He mixed the dried milk with the water. He would hand it three times a day to the young camel. Sores and scabs began to appear on its body. The boy Rashid suffered from nightmares.

'The camel has eaten me,' he would cry in his sleep. 'It's chewed off my arm. It's chewed off my leg.'

Relations between Abdulla and his wife worsened over this young camel. She no longer cooked him his favourite food. She had a headache most evenings. There was no alternative. The young camel had to go.

The Camel of the Quarter

Abdulla released the scabby thin young camel. It stood for a while outside Abdulla's front door and then began to wander off round the streets and alleys of the quarter, Jafiliya. He ate from rubbish skips and slept in the recesses of the alley ways. The boys and youths of the quarter got to know him. He often used to stand near

Abud's grocery, a general meeting place. They gave him the name Pepsi because he would take a Pepsi bottle they gave him in his mouth, raise it up, drain all its contents and then throw it away.

They used to give him sweets, biscuits, dates and bread. They also used to call him Smoker because one lad would blow cigarette smoke into his face and they reckoned he enjoyed its smell.

For several months Pepsi remained the public property of all the lads who sat round Abud's grocery. Each one used to give him a piece of biscuit or a sweet or some drink. All of them used to play with him and get on his back when he was crouching. When he got up they would fall off. Sometimes they would make him kick a football. And when Al Nasr football team won they would decorate him with blue garlands on his feet and round his neck.

Farhan and Pepsi

Farhan Said was a black man in his forties. He used to work on an oil rig carrying pipes. On a very hot day of a very hot summer he was slow in grabbing one of the huge iron pipes. It swung around and struck him hard on the side and knocked him out. Farhan's pelvic bone was broken. The helicopter that transported the workers to the mainland was delayed. When he reached the hospital he was in a critical state. He stayed there six months. An official of the company assured him that he would get generous compensation but when he came out of hospital he received only seven thousand riyals.

After that accident whenever he went anywhere his movements were a mixture of walking, limping and creeping. He tried to be a ferryman but was unable to manage. He tried his luck in business but failed. He helped to provide services for wedding parties in return for a few dirhams but was not successful. He withdrew to drinking Cleopatra perfume in which he found solace and peace. Most of his time he spent near Abud's grocery. When they made a record of those in need at the Ministry of Social Affairs the young men took him to the Ministry so his name could be registered. Every three months they took him to the Ministry so he could get his allowance. They then brought him back to his base and his bottle.

Farhan's permanent base near Abud's grocery made him get to

know Pepsi better than anyone else. When he was very drunk Farhan would confide all his troubles to Pepsi.

'Life's a bitch. I used to be the strongest workman of all and carry the heaviest pipes. The American engineer was always saying, "Farhan very good, very good. Farhan very strong." Today I cannot even carry my own body.'

'There was this whore. I used to take her a bottle of whisky. Whisky was worth something then, but not today when even kids drink the stuff.'

'I've got to submit a claim against the Company. The compensation they gave me was pathetic. Thieves. Robbers.'

'Look. Look at that dog, Salum. My mother brought him up in filth and piss after his mother threw him out and ran away with a driver and went off to Abu Dhabi. Now he passes by and doesn't even say "Hello". The dog is as arrogant as shit.'

With the passage of time the intimacy between Farhan and Pepsi increased and Farhan used to take Pepsi to his one-roomed house. Farhan usually slept outside in the narrow courtyard. The lads who gathered round Abud's grocery raised no objection when Pepsi left their common property and became the possession of Farhan. Indeed they were quite pleased. Over the months Pepsi had put on weight and got plump. He recovered from the scabs thanks to the diet of dates, bread, sweets, fruit and bottles of mineral water. When Pepsi sat for long periods of time without moving near the grocery one of the lads observed, 'It looks as if Pepsi has been drinking Cleopatra with Farhan.'

'He'll be the first camel to be an alcoholic,' another lad said.

A third chuckled.

'No, this is the first camel to enjoy his tipple.'

Farhan would laugh but he was inwardly hurt at these remarks.

The Dream of Racing

One day one lad smiled at Farhan as he looked at Pepsi.

'Why don't you enter him for the camel races?' he said.

'Pepsi join in the camel races!' Farhan laughed. 'I don't want him to tire himself out.'

Another lad liked the idea and said, 'Pepsi is a tough camel. If he wins he will get a prize of 100,000 dirhams.'

The lads went on to talk about camels and racing.

'When we were in Shindagha,' one of them said, 'there was a camel race on the first day of the marriage of one of the merchants. He was from a Bedu family and traded in animals. It was the custom to put scented saffron on the camel that won. The bride's aunt put some tomato paste on the winning camel. The Bedu who took part in the race complained and there was a row.'

Another lad told another story. Farhan thought about 100,000 dirhams. What a sum. How could he get his hands on it? What would he do with it? He would build a huge house and provide special quarters for Pepsi. He would buy a Landrover and get a chauffeur to drive Pepsi and himself around. He would buy crates of whisky instead of the bottles of the foul perfume he was used to drinking. He would buy cigarettes and drinks every day for the lads at Abud's grocery.

Next day Farhan talked to the lads about Pepsi joining in the official camel races. Some of them laughed and there were a number of reactions.

'How can your camel that drinks Pepsi Cola compete with strong camels that are fed on honey and cow's milk?'

'Some camels that take part in the races are Sudanese and can run faster than horses.'

'The camels are trained for the races. Your camel is sluggish and can hardly shift from the store to the rubbish tip.'

'Racing camels are sleek and almost fly along the race track. Pepsi is as fat as a buffalo.'

These remarks had no effect on Farhan's daydreams. Some of what the lads said pointed out the path to follow to get Pepsi to the race track. He began to buy for his camel bottles of cow's milk and tins of honey from the nearby Indian supermarket. He lay in wait for the lads who used to give Pepsi an apple or a biscuit or a sweet and tried to restrain them from these habits of kindness towards Pepsi. Some took no notice and went on giving Pepsi bits of biscuits or sweetmeats. He would swallow them with speed and with gusto. As soon as Farhan saw what was going on he picked up a small stick, hobbled after the lads and beat them. Some would blow cigarette smoke into the face of Pepsi who obviously enjoyed it. Farhan went mad and cursed them.

'Sons of bitches. Leave Pepsi alone. The smoke will do him harm. Why don't you blow smoke into your mothers' faces?'

Farhan was drinking less perfume. He was training Pepsi for the race track. It was a hilarious sight for all the lads to watch Farhan limp along leading Pepsi from Abud's grocery to the Satwa fire station roundabout, on to the Trade Centre and then come back behind the police station and across the open space south of the district and then return to Abud's grocery. When they reached the store after each of these outings his feet were dusty and he was out of breath. But joy and happiness lit up his face. He would drink half a bottle of mineral water and give the other half to Pepsi who lifted the bottle up over his head. When he had finished it he threw it on to the ground.

Most of the youths laughed at Farhan's hope of entering Pepsi for the camel races. Some sympathised. None believed Pepsi would have a chance even if by a miracle he were to enter.

Before prayers one evening Pepsi was going from Abud's grocery to one of the rubbish skips, taking no notice of Farhan who was sleeping off an unaccustomed amount of perfume. An American car driven by a youngster came along at high speed. The driver suddenly saw Pepsi and tried to swerve and avoid him. The car struck Pepsi on his hind legs. Pepsi fell to one side. The car collided with a rubbish skip and sent it flying. Farhan woke up in a state of shock at all this noise. The driver was frightened and drove on even though the car had a damaged bonnet. Farhan hurried over with one lad to Pepsi. They tried to raise him but were unable to. A stream of curses poured forth from Farhan, mingled with cries of grief and distress.

'Curse you. Dog. Poor dear Pepsi. Where's the police? Where's the law?'

Other youths ran up. After heroic efforts they managed to get Pepsi to Farhan's house and helped him put some salt and local medicine on his feet. Farhan stayed at home with Pepsi for three weeks. He gave up his hopes for the races but he did not want Pepsi to die. After the third week Pepsi was able to move a little and eat with more appetite.

Pepsi now comes with Farhan to Abud's grocery and limps as he limps. The lads have gone back to feeding Pepsi with biscuits, sweets and fruit and bottles of Pepsi which he lifts up with his mouth and drains and then throws away. And some lads have gone back to blowing cigarette smoke into the face of Pepsi who enjoys it. Farhan looks on and lives up to his own name which means happy.

4
Pleasures of the Night

Jasim stopped his car by the Golan cafeteria and sounded the horn. The Indian boy asked him what he wanted to order. Jasim asked what there was. The Indian boy began to run through a list of juices – grape, cocktail, orange, pineapple, mango, banana, pomegranate . . . Jasim stopped him and said, 'Give me some pomegranate juice'. He had eaten a heavy dinner, for his wife had cooked him a thick chicken broth which he loved. And from the house of a neighbour where the daughter had just got married they had had some harisa and grilled meat with rice flavoured with saffron, cardamon and cinnamon and other spices. One of his friends had told him that pomegranate juice was good for the digestion for it helped heavy meals go down.

As he was waiting for the juice he saw in front of him a white Toyota. Its driver, a young man, had got out and was showing his mates the many extras that had been fitted on and which made the car like one of those space rockets he had seen on television. The young driver had long hair that came down to his shoulders and which was cut in the style of Michael Jackson. How that young man must get tired of washing and combing it. Either that or he would be suffering from a scabby scalp. When the pain of scabs was added to long hair then God help him with the huge job of washing and cleaning it.

Jasim switched the car radio on. The local radio station was broadcasting a programme for music fans. An ugly voice hit his ear and he switched over to another station broadcasting a programme of hints for farmers. He turned the radio off and put on a tape. The voice of Umm Kulthum came over, quietly exuberant, strong and tender. It harmonised opposites and made the heart dance. He thought of his wife who loved the songs of Umm Kulthum. She was in the eighth month of her pregnancy and was an unfamiliar shape. When she wore her flowing maternity dresses, decorated with many colours, and walked with her hands behind her back she looked like an enormous ball. His friend, Abdullah, told him that he had fallen for a pregnant woman in Sanadiq suq. She had been responsive and he had gone on seeing her after the confinement. Abdullah had not been in touch with him for a while, certainly not since the time the rent for the flat was due. Three friends had clubbed together to take the flat, each paying three thousand dirhams every six months. It was Abdullah who paid the sum to the landlord, organised the furniture and the cleaning and kept the fridge full of food and drink.

The Indian boy brought the pomegranate juice. The glass had a strange shape and looked like some laboratory equipment that Jasim remembered from his schooldays. Jasim did not use the flat as much as the others. Pleasures of the night cost a lot of money. Jasim did not like to spend and use up his money buying presents. He once bought a gold watch for a fleeting girlfriend that cost two thousand dirhams. For long afterwards he suffered from remorse for that lapse. Abdullah had a girlfriend who loved him but did not demand presents, but often bought him valuable gifts. Khalifa had lots of girlfriends but he was a spendthrift and threw money away to please them and to keep their affection for him. He finished the pomegranate juice and saw three boys seize a small dog and try to cut off the end of its tail with a knife. The dog was yelping with pain and terror. Jasim could not bear to watch. He switched on the ignition and quietly left the place.

He drove to Burj Nahar Roundabout and did a complete circle around it. He went back to the streets of downtown Deira. At one corner he saw a young woman coming out of a side street, walking slowly. He slowed down until he was alongside her. He became bold all of a sudden. He said in a voice that tried to be both strong and gentle, 'Can I take you anywhere?'

She stopped walking, turned towards him, came up to the car window and said in a strange voice, 'Is there anybody with you?'

He was taken aback by this question, especially as his car was a small sports model with only two seats, but he replied, 'No. Do get in.'

Jasim leant over to open the passenger door. The girl got inside. Jasim set off at speed. He was thrilled at how easy it all was. There was a strong smell of perfume. There was no doubt that she was on the game. Not that it mattered. It had been a dull evening and he would pay her. He would not pay a lot but he would pay what she wanted so long as it was reasonable. She would not make any excessive demands for she could see that his car was a modest one, that he was wearing a cheap Japanese watch and did not have a gold ring studded with diamonds and expensive jewels. These girls were intelligent and were able to sum up the value of a client with a glance at the car and the clothes. Jasim set off for the flat feeling very pleased with himself.

II

As they drove along, the young lady did not say much. She observed, 'There's a lot of cloud about. It's going to rain soon.'

Jasim replied, 'I hope so. We haven't had any rain for a long time.'

Jasim stopped at the traffic lights by the Fish Monument Roundabout near Claridge's Hotel. She said, 'These fish have died in spite of all the water around.'

Jasim did not know what to make of this odd remark. He tried to think of something polite to say and replied, 'Umm Kulthum says in her song from the Rubaiyat of Omar Khayyam, "Oh, my Lord, are you content with this thirst while all around me water is pouring down in torrents?"'

She said with a smile, 'I'm thirsty.'

Jasim replied, 'We'll go to the flat and you can drink whatever you want.'

She said, her face anxious again, 'After that you'll take me home?'

He replied quickly, 'Of course. Of course.'

There was a short silence. Jasim looked at her face, quite firm, her lips slender and her eyes sweet, her dress modest. She could have been an ordinary girl who wanted a bit of an adventure, who wanted to break the routine of the life she led or to escape from

25

some tyrannical stepmother. He reproached himself for imagining that she was a lady of pleasure. Up to now she had made no demands on him. She had not put those practical questions he was accustomed to hear from such women. She must obviously be merchandise of a different sort, something new which he had not come across in his life before, an interesting diversion for the night. Jasim was filled with feelings of happiness and was anticipating delights ahead of him. He put his foot on the accelerator and drove off at over a hundred kilometres an hour, something he had not done before. He switched the radio on. The news was over and the announcer was wishing her listeners a good night. The girl stretched out her hand and switched the radio off and asked, 'What's your name?'

The question took him by surprise and he replied mechanically, 'Jasim'.

He regretted his answer later. Why did he not give her some other name as he usually did with women whom in the past he had casually picked up in order to relieve boredom?

She asked him, 'Do you dream much?'

He was taken aback by the question but answered, 'No. I only rarely dream and then not much.'

She said, looking into Jasim's face, 'I dream a lot. When I dream I see lots of birds and beasts and fish. Last night I dreamt that I was on the beach and a great whale came and swallowed me up. In his huge inside I found a bed and some armchairs and a television. After a long while it spewed me up on the beach of one of the islands and there an enormous eagle carried me on its back and flew ever so high. We passed over seas that were yellow, green, red and grey. After a while he set me down on the top of a white mountain. I then came down from the summit to a forest swarming with snakes that invited me to live with them. One of the snakes was mottled in colour and had three eyes. It did not welcome my presence and cursed me. When I wanted to answer back my mother woke me up.'

Jasim said with a laugh, 'If your mother had not woken you up that mottled snake would have bitten you.'

The girl did not laugh at this remark. She remained silent. They were almost at the block where the flat was. Right from the beginning Jasim had not been happy about its location. It was in the middle of the Hamriya quarter where a lot of families lived.

Jasim would have preferred it to have been in one of those quarters inhabited by bachelors and foreign workers. But Abdullah had insisted. He said it belonged to a friend of his who had looked after their interests as far as the rent was concerned. The flat was spacious and had large bedrooms. It overlooked the sea and they were able to enjoy watching the waves of the Gulf.

They reached the buildings. There was no light on in the flat but Jasim wanted to make quite sure and said to the girl, 'Wait here a couple of minutes, please, while I check there's nobody in the flat.'

The girl said, 'But I'm thirsty.'

Jasim replied enthusiastically, 'Just two minutes and then we can drink ourselves silly.'

Jasim went to the lift. It was out of order. He used the stairs. The flat was on the third floor. He got there, panting, opened the door and put on the lights. A smell of lingering cigarette smoke gave the flat a stale atmosphere. He raced to the kitchen, took the air freshener and sprayed all the rooms and especially the bedroom. The bedding had not been changed for some time and there were some large stains on it. Jasim stripped the bed and put the bedding in the wardrobe, replacing it with a fresh counterpane and pillows. He adjusted the large cushions in the sitting room and checked that the fridge was full. He went down the stairs quietly to avoid rousing the neighbours. Before he reached the car the sound of Umm Kulthum came blaring out from the car cassette player. He ran to the car, pounced on the player and switched it off and said in confusion, 'Why did you put that on so loudly?'

'I was bored. You were taking such a long time.'

He said warily, 'My dear, we are in a residential area and don't want any problems.'

He smiled and added, 'Now let's go up to the flat for a drink and make ourselves at home.'

III

When they got into the flat the girl tossed her aba'a casually on to one of the cushions on the living-room floor and went over to the television and switched it on. Jasim felt reassured because she was behaving so naturally as if she was at home. He took off his ghutra and iqal. The girl's eyes were glued to the television screen. The heroine in some series was talking with her lover who was promising marriage. Jasim asked her, 'What would you like to drink?'

She replied without turning her head, 'Pepsi Cola'.

He went to the fridge and opened it. There was no Pepsi Cola, only Double Cola. He took one out and also a can of beer. He placed them on a tray with a couple of glasses and also one plate of nuts and raisins and another with pieces of cheese and some olives. When he took the tray back into the living room he found the girl in tears. He put the tray on the floor and asked her with some anxiety why she was crying. She wiped the tears away with her hand and said, 'Adil isn't going to marry Laila. He's given in to the pressure of his hard hearted brother.'

Jasim was puzzled. 'Who is this Adil?'

She replied with some surprise, 'Adil in the TV serial. Didn't you know that?'

Jasim smiled at this reply. His smile turned to loud laughter and he spluttered a reply. 'You got me worried a bit with your crying. I thought it was something in real life.'

She gave him a look of astonishment and said indignantly, 'You've got no heart.'

He answered, trying to justify himself, 'But the TV series is just play acting.'

She replied in all seriousness, 'But Laila was crying with real tears.'

Jasim did not want to carry on an argument on the subject. He reached out for the beer and the girl asked, 'What's that?'

'A can of beer.'

'I want one like yours.'

Jasim smiled, got up and went to the kitchen. After a moment he came back with another can of beer and gave it to her. She opened it and poured it into a glass until it was half full. She then opened the can of Double Cola and poured that into the beer until it reached the top of the glass. Jasim watched with some surprise and said with a mixture of bafflement and disapproval, 'You should drink beer by itself without mixing it with other drinks.'

'Who says so?'

'It's well known. Everybody drinks beer like that. You mix

28

whisky with water or something else.'

'I want to drink beer the way they drink whisky. I'm free to drink as I please.'

'Yes, but . . .'

She interrupted him by asking, 'Where's the bathroom?'

He showed her where the bathroom was and said, 'The light switch is just to the right of the door.'

Jasim began to go over in his mind what the girl had said. Some of her remarks were strange – and also her behaviour. What was the reason for that? Was she one of those feminists – he had seen one of them talking on a television programme. He reckoned she had been one of those Amazonian warriors who hated men. Perhaps she was a drug addict. Khalifa had told him that a girlfriend of his had been an addict, but that she was an amazing girl and very compliant. The world had become very strange. Nobody knew what to expect from women or from men. The girl came out of the bathroom. She had let down her hair which had been pinned up at the back of her head. It now poured down on to her shoulders. This flowing black cascade took away all Jasim's apprehensions and restored his optimistic expectations for an interesting and pleasurable night. She came and sat down next to him. She took his hand and placed it in her palm and said with a laugh, 'Your hand is small and your fingers are tiny. My hand is bigger than yours.'

Jasim said, smiling, 'My father's hands were small.'

She saw the cassette player by the television, got up and went to it and said, 'Have you got any of the songs of Ali al Rawgha or Muhid Hamad?'

'I've got tapes of Umm Kulthum, Abdul Wahhab, Abdul Halim and Warda and I suppose there's an old tape of Ali al Rawgha.'

She rummaged among the tapes. After a while she found something she wanted and put it in the player and turned the knob to full volume. The flat vibrated with the noise of flute and drum and singing. Jasim leapt to the player and quickly turned it down saying with some annoyance, 'What on earth are you doing? Do you want to draw people's attention to us?'

'Why should people be bothered about us? Darling, aren't we free agents in our lives?'

He replied less angrily, 'True, but . . .'

'We'll get married shortly and take our honeymoon in India.'

Jasim was bowled over by the reference to marriage which was quite out of the blue. He did not know what to say. The girl went on talking.

'Would you prefer India or Cairo? When my auntie got married she went to Cairo.'

Jasim's calm was very much disturbed by such talk. The girl went on talking on the same theme.

'I don't want to get pregnant in the first year. My sister did so and she was sick and dizzy for months on end. Do you love children?'

The question took Jasim aback and he answered, 'Kids are sweet.'

'I will have a lot of sweet children for you to love.'

Jasim did not know whether the girl was being serious or whether she was making fun of him with talk like this. He took her right hand and said, 'Don't you think talk of marriage is a little premature?'

She quickly withdrew her hand from his and said angrily, 'You want to abandon me just like Adil did to Laila. You men are all the same. Betrayers and deceivers. You've got no conscience and no idea of fidelity.'

She was choked by her tears and began to cry distressingly and noisily. Jasim was embarrassed by the tears. She suddenly stopped crying and said, 'It's hot in here. Why don't you put the AC on?'

'But it's January.'

'That doesn't matter. The heat is suffocating. Switch the AC on.'

'All right, all right.'

He went to the air conditioning and turned it on.

At least the noise would drown her crying and her loud voice. She stood up and said, 'I haven't had a bath for a whole month. I'll just take a quick shower.'

She disappeared into the bathroom. Jasim was overcome with confusion and anxiety. He began to go over what she had said and what she had done. She was certainly unbalanced. She was schizophrenic or hysterical. What was he going to do now? He would have to do his best to let the night pass peacefully. A little later she appeared at the door wrapped in the huge towel that had been in the bathroom. It had on it the picture of a nude woman. The girl's hair was wet. The shower had washed away her make-up and face powder but the kohl that seemed to be very thick still traced dark lines down her cheeks. Her face looked like that of a clown he had seen in the World Circus Programme on television. She came up to him and said, 'Would you like me to dance in front of you naked?'

Had this suggestion been made in any other circumstances Jasim would have been overjoyed. He would have pounced on the cassette player to put on a tape of oriental dance music. But on this occasion he was scared at the suggestion. He said in a tone that betrayed his anxiety, 'No. I don't want you to do that.'

She said with surprise, 'Why not?'

He said, stuttering, 'Your head is wet and the AC is on. You'll catch a fever.'

She came straight to him, kissed him on the head and said, 'Oh, my love, you're worried about my health.'

He said, full of embarrassment, 'Yes, my dear. I'm worried about your health. Go and get dressed.'

'OK, darling. Yes, my husband.'

She ran off to the bathroom. What a ghastly situation. Husband again. What could he do in this crisis? He was crazy. Why did he stop for her in the first place? Why did he bring her to the flat? Why had he not taken his pregnant wife for a walk by the Creek? The gynaecologist had said that walking was good for her. Why did he not go and call on his mother? He had not seen her for a long while. He was not a very dutiful son. His brother Salim went to see her ever day. What was he going to do now? He had to act calmly. It was up to him to persuade her that the party was over and that they must leave the flat. She appeared from the bathroom and had put her dress on. She had dried her hair a bit but her face was still stained with lines of thick black kohl. She asked, 'Where's the kitchen?'

He replied in a tone of alarm as he thought of the knives there. 'What do you want in the kitchen?'

She quietly answered, 'I want to cook us some dinner.'

He said uneasily, 'What, you want to cook . . . ?'

'Yes. I'm hungry and you're hungry and it's the wife's duty to cook for her husband . . .'

He said, trying to put her off. 'But there's no meat in the fridge . . . There's a chicken that has been frozen for a long time and I don't suppose it's fit to be cooked or eaten. You have to boil

31

it a long time before it's all right . . . And we haven't got any spices . . . and there aren't any . . .'

She cut him off with the words, 'I love chicken and we can wait.'

He glanced at his watch with exasperation, 'It's a quarter to one now.'

'It doesn't matter. And we can borrow some spices from next door.'

He interrupted her and said, 'I will not let you borrow spices from next door.'

'Never mind. I'll cook without spices.'

He said, trying to sound calm and affectionate, 'My dear, I don't want to trouble you with cooking and its problems. Let's go to a restaurant and take away a nice tasty meal and after that we'll go to the road by the Creek and have our meal quietly and watch the lights of the buildings reflected in the water.'

The girl smiled and said, 'My love, you are sensitive and poetic. Let's go.'

On the stairs down she whistled loudly. Jasim hoped that none of the neighbours could hear this disturbing noise. When they settled into the car, she suddenly said, 'I've left my aba'a in the flat. I'll slip back and get it.'

He said, pleadingly, 'Please, stay here in the car. I'll go and fetch it.'

After a couple of minutes Jasim brought back the aba'a. The engine started up and Jasim breathed a sigh of relief.

IV

Jasim went to one of the restaurants in the Manama district. He stopped the car and sounded the horn. An Arab lad who worked there came out and said, 'Welcome, welcome friends. Your presence brightens up the restaurant. My hands are at your service.'

The girl laughed aloud and said, 'We don't want to eat your hands. I shouldn't imagine they're very tasty. Maybe your brain . . . Ha ha ha! My husband and I want a roast chicken. Ha ha ha! But without the feathers or fluff. Ha ha ha!'

The lad said, 'Fine. Fine. Fine. At your service.'

Jasim was cringing with embarrassment at the girl's words, but what the hell! The people working in the restaurant did not know him.

The lad went to his colleague who prepared the take-away orders and said disapprovingly, 'Nowadays women get drunk. Wine is OK for men but it's not the thing for women.'

Jasim switched the radio on. It was broadcasting an old song of Suad Muhammad. The girl said, 'This is Umm Kulthum.'

Jasim did not want any argument, so said, 'Yes. It's Umm Kulthum.'

He looked at the car clock which said half past one. His wife was sure to be very anxious about him being late. Maybe she would get in touch with his brother Salim or with his friends Abdullah or Khalifa. And who knows? She may contact the police. She was a woman as crazy as this girl who was gazing at the lights of the restaurant. Women were all completely crazy but they were crazy at different levels. The lad was taking his time bringing out the chicken. Jasim sounded the car horn. From the restaurant the lad put his hands and spread out all his fingers to indicate that it would take ten more minutes. This was a frightful restaurant. The ten minutes stretched to twenty. His companion stared at the restaurant lights and would now and then surprise him with one or other of her disconcerting observations:

'Did you know you can get cancer from eating carrots?'

'They say the Municipality is going to pull down all the houses in our quarter except our house.'

'I don't like green cars.'

'Did you know I love reading picture magazines?'

'My aunt is younger than I am and has been married for two years.'

Jasim made no comment on these remarks beyond gruffly mumbling a few broken words. Finally they brought the chicken, bread, salad and humus. Jasim drove the car quickly towards the Creek. Ten minutes later they reached the road by the Creek just by the Town Hall. He stopped the car near the sailing boats, the dhows and the small craft moored to the right bank of the Creek. There was nobody about. Most of the sailors were asleep aboard their craft and others were sleeping on the quayside.

The girl opened the paper bag they had brought from the restaurant. There was the aroma of grilled chicken. The girl tore off one of the legs and dunked it in the humus and started to chew

33

at it. Jasim dipped a piece of bread in the humus and ate it slowly. He looked at the still waters of the Creek and then at his car clock. It was after two o'clock in the morning. He was overcome with feelings of misery and despair. His eyes filled with tears which poured down his cheeks and became mixed up in his mouth with the bread and humus.

5

The Long-Awaited Trip

The last time Jamila went on a journey was four years ago when she went with her family to Cyprus and London. Three months after that delightful holiday she got engaged to Hamid and six months later married him. He did not take her on a honeymoon because his mother did not approve of such ridiculous new fangled ideas. She had not even wanted to hold a women's party at a hotel on the night of the wedding, such parties being wretched innovations. If it had not been for the insistent pleadings of her son and the enormous efforts put in by her sisters to persuade Hamid's mother, she would have been satisfied with just a dinner party at home in accordance with her principles and tradition. She was the only woman at the hotel party who did not smile all evening in spite of all the other happy laughing faces. In the few photographs that were taken of her with the bride and groom she was scowling and glowering as though seething with anger, vindictiveness and discontent.

Jamila became pregnant in the first month. The result, nine months later, was a bonny dark lass whom Jamila wanted to call Hanan. When her mother-in-law heard of this innocent maternal wish she exploded with anger.

'You've wanted to have your own way right from the beginning. This is quite impossible. Hanan is an absurd name which has been brought in with all these other strange new names. She will be called Adhija after my late grandmother.'

Jamila recovered from the effects of childbirth and got her resilience back. Then when her daughter was only five months old she felt the pains, fatigues, and sickness and all the indications of a fresh pregnancy. The Egyptian lady doctor confirmed the pregnancy and said with a smile, 'Congratulations, a little brother will come to amuse and play with Adhija.'

Jamila was upset. She was hoping to have a rest for a couple of years to bring Adhija up in a modern way, following the best advice she had read in many of the books about bringing up children which she had collected and read during her pregnancy. Also she wanted to spend time with her husband and to travel with him especially as her happy memories of her last trip with her family to Cyprus and London were still vivid in her mind: the beach at Limassol full of cheerful fun, its restaurants teeming with tasty dishes, Hyde Park in London and its big lake and its rowing boats in which she had rowed with her little sister and her cousin, the bean sandwich and shawarma at Marouche's in the Edgware Road, the huge amazing fascinating department stores in Oxford Street: all these places came back to her mind in the tedious and draining days and months of her pregnancy. She would feel gusts of fresh air especially when she thought that she might go to those places again with her husband.

When the second baby arrived she did not offer any suggestion for his name. She had learnt her lesson the first time round. Her mother-in-law was satisfied with this wifely compliance and said with an air of condescension, 'We'll call him Khalifa after Jamila's grandfather!'

II

When Khalifa was toddling Jamila entertained hopes of travel once more. She knew that her husband was very busy in the small construction business he owned and that he did not travel a lot, but she started to talk to him about her desire in a roundabout way.

'My sister a couple of days ago went off on a month's holiday with her husband.'

'Our neighbours went to Cairo yesterday.'

'It's hot and humid in Dubai this year.'

'When a man goes on a journey he renews his strength and is fit for work.'

Her husband recognised all these hints but took no notice because he was immersed in his job, managing the project of building a small primary school for the Ministry of Education. There was a shortfall in the workforce and the contract contained a heavy penalty clause for delays in completing the project.

Jamila switched to a direct approach.

'Hamid, my love, why don't we travel somewhere. Since we got married we haven't been away once. Every couple has memories of the countries they have been to together except us.'

'But you were pregnant for two whole years.'

'Was that my fault?'

'No, it wasn't your fault, but that was the situation.'

'Well, it's no longer the situation. Adhija is a little devil and Khalifa is a young rascal, the Lord be praised. He's always tearing magazines to pieces and he can't touch a plant in a pot without pulling all its leaves off.'

'Fine, but what do we do with the children?'

'We'll leave them with my mother.'

'My mother won't like that.'

'Then let her take them.'

'Where would you like to go to?'

Jamila was overjoyed when she heard this. It meant that Hamid was beginning to be open to the idea. She wanted to suggest Cyprus and London but she did not want to seem to be determining the course of events. She said, putting as much gentleness and love into her voice as she could, 'Any place, my dearest, that you take me to will be lovely.'

Hamid thought for a little while and said decisively, 'Right. We'll go to Bombay for ten days.'

Jamila was taken aback and said in some confusion, 'Bombay?!'

Hamid replied in a serious and practical way, 'Yes, Bombay, a fine beautiful city. I know it well for I've been there half a dozen times or more and I speak Hindi. Moreover the trip can be partly business as I'll bring back some workers I need to finish the primary school in the time stipulated without incurring a fine.'

Jamila did not want to offer any resistance or to argue with him in the choice of city that he would take her to. After all she had not thought it possible to persuade him to travel at all and here he was, persuaded, and choosing the place and the length of stay. The time was not too bad for she did not think she could bear to be away from the children for more than ten days. But the destination: Bombay. She reflected on the matter. Those few friends of hers who had been to Bombay did not talk much about the city. All their talk was about frankincense and joss sticks and embroidered silk Indian dresses. She remembered the Indian films she had seen on television. Most of them were quite fascinating and revolved around the adventures of thieves and gangs and tales of love and passion with lots of sentimental songs. And the location of the events of the film were majestic alluring places . . . palaces, fountains, gardens, lakes, places of amusement. When the date for the long-awaited journey was fixed, she embarked on a series of telephone conversations with her sisters, her women friends and relations. 'Hamid and I are off to Bombay, the city of incense and attar, of magic, of dreams and of beauty. This is the first time we'll have been away and Hamid has selected a lovely place full of poetry for which he has the happiest memories because he's been there heaps of times. We'll be flying at night, which will be relaxing and calm, a time for pleasant dreams.'

III

A quarter of an hour after the plane took off Jamila had a bit of a headache which did not leave her until a few seconds before touching down at Bombay airport. The English hostesses were extremely rude and arrogant. They were held up a long time at the airport, at passport control and at the customs. The road from the airport was depressing. Dawn was beginning to break. She could not see anything out of the small dark window of the taxi they rode in. There were just different shades of grey. Slowly the colour of trees and green plants could be made out. Then the colour of the ground and human beings who were brownish black. There was no airconditioning in the taxi and the oppressive humidity weighed heavily upon them. A foul smelling breeze met them as they approached the city. Jamila felt cross. They reached the Taj Mahal Hotel. Her husband filled in the hotel forms and within half an hour they had collapsed into a deep sleep.

Jamila woke up at twelve noon. She felt uncomfortable all over because of the change of bed and the stress of the journey. She cautiously opened the window. Their room overlooked the coast of the Arabian sea. It was cloudy and to the right some thick dark clouds could be seen. Further away she could see ships of the Navy, smaller craft and three separate islands. The sea was grey and turbulent. She recalled the blue and green colours of the Gulf and felt homesick.

After breakfast they went for a walk among the bazaars of Coloba. Jamila saw some cheap garishly coloured handwork goods, some ill-cut and badly tailored clothes, sickly poverty-stricken dark faces and child beggars, their faces full of disfigure-ments, trying to force her to buy garlands of jasmine. Women beggars were seizing her by the sleeve of her aba'a. Men were leaving restaurants after lunch and spitting on to the narrow pavement the red chewing stuff that Indians ate after meals to freshen their breath. When they reached a shop a young Indian shopkeeper grabbed her camera and said insistently, 'How much do you want for this camera?'

Jamila was terrified and looked fearfully at her husband who told the man off and informed him that their cameras were not for sale. In these streets they saw third and fourth class hotels in front of which people were sitting and staring at the passers-by. The frightful stench of the alleys made Jamila choke. She asked her husband if they could go back to the hotel.

That night her husband went to have dinner with a friend from Sharjah whom he had met in the hotel foyer. Jamila had dinner by herself and sobbed a lot.

Next day she asked her husband if they could sit in the hall that overlooked the hotel swimming pool. She liked the white columns and the green wood and leather armchairs, and the huge old white roof fans. She wanted to sit with her husband on the comfortable wooden swing to the right of the hall. At first he hesitated. He was afraid lest a compatriot staying in the hotel might see him, but she tearfully insisted and he agreed. They sat down on the swing. The pool was full of Japanese tourists, men and women. Her husband asked the waiter to get them a couple of glasses of lemonade and some cheese and lettuce sandwiches. The heat and the humidity intensified. When the snacks arrived three cats came out from beneath the armchairs. Two were white and marmalade and the third was white with an ugly head. The cats started to mew plaintively and unceasingly. It was a disturbing racket that stopped only when Jamila tossed some sandwich at them. A little while after that it began to rain and all the Japanese tourists fled to the chairs inside the hall except for one girl who took no notice of the rain and carried on swimming in the pool, exposed to the water beneath her and the water above as if she wanted to drown in it all. An old man from Dubai came into the hall with a young lad. They passed near the pool and saw Hamid and Jamila sitting on the swing. Hamid was furious all of a sudden and whispered angrily to her, 'You've caused a scandal. The man is from Dubai.'

Jamila asked crossly, 'What's the scandal?'

'My God, don't you realise? They've seen us on this swing.'

'So what? Are we naked or behaving immodestly?'

Hamid asked for the bill, quickly settled it and mumbled angrily, 'It's a mistake to listen to women.'

The day had begun badly. Hamid spent the rest of the day with the representative of an employment agency and did not get back until evening. Jamila did not leave her room. She watched three films on the hotel television, a cowboy film, an American detective film and a romantic English film most of which was dialogue which she could not follow.

On the morning of the third day her husband said to her, 'Today we'll go where all the women who visit Bombay love to go.'

A taxi took them through narrow streets and alleyways until they reached a road near the fruit and vegetable market. They went into a building with faintly coloured walls outside. Then up a narrow flight of stairs and into a wide room full of white cushions with back rests and soothing decoration. The place was crowded with women from the Gulf and Indian salesmen. They sat on the floor near one of the salesmen. He smiled and said to them, 'Yes. What do you want? Embroidered dresses, jallabiyas, silk cloth, cotton cloth, pullovers, shawls?'

She asked to see some dresses and jallabiyas. There were laid out in front of Jamila and Hamid dozens of embroidered dresses and brocaded jallabiyas. Most of those that Jamila liked did not please Hamid. He kept on making negative comments:

'The decoration on this dress is a bit heavy and you won't be able to walk in it.'

'This jallabiya is too red to calm the nerves.'

'This dress is full of colours that clash.'

'This jallabiya is made of cloth that is light and transparent. It's scandalous.'

She selected a number of dresses and jallabiyas that fitted in with her husband's taste. The time came to pay. Her husband argued at length with the salesman. He argued vigorously and violently.

'Those prices are inflated. You're thieves, you're robbers.'

When the salesman made only a small discount, he turned to wheadling and pleading.

'You reckon everyone coming from the Gulf is rich. That's not true. We're poor.'

Jamila deplored what her husband was saying and felt acutely embarrassed, especially when she caught sight of a group of her elder sister's friends stealing glances at her husband and looking at him when he first made demands and followed that by trying to ingratiate.

The same drama was repeated at the perfume shop. There Jamila was even more embarrassed because she saw an aunt with a friend. When the haggling was over, there was a smile of triumph on her husband's face, even though the discount he had obtained after all the tiresome negotiation was trifling.

In the evening they went for a walk along the Corniche near the Gateway to India. Jamila saw people selling grilled maize and asked her husband to buy some for her. The man poured salt and squeezed lemon on it. That night Jamila suffered acute pains in her stomach. The disturbances inside her reminded her of the pain and discomfort of pregnancy.

The following day her husband said to her, 'Today we'll go to Elephanta Island. The boat trip is a delight.'

Jamila put on her best dress and took her best handbag made from crocodile leather. They boarded the boat at the Gateway to India. It soon became packed with passengers. The sea was calm. The boat set off. Half an hour later the huge buildings of the city seemed like small matchboxes far away. They reached Elephanta Island. Jamila saw no elephants but she did see countless troops of monkeys of all shapes and sizes. They went into a huge cave with a statue of one of the Hindu gods with three faces. When they sat at a wooden table for a rest beneath a huge tree one of the monkeys slipped down and pinched Jamila's handbag and ran away with it to the top of the tree. There he started to throw out all the contents of the bag – combs, powder boxes, kohl pens, lipstick, a bottle of nail varnish and other items of make-up. It tore or broke everything with its teeth and nails. It then ripped up the bag, tearing off the handle and threw it all away. Jamila was being assailed by disaster after disaster. She cursed the unsettling and unfriendly Elephanta Island. On the return journey the sea was rough and Jamila felt fear and loathing. She also had a headache from watching other passengers suffering from sea sickness.

On the last day Jamila had had enough. The whole trip had been full of problems and irritations. Air pollution had discoloured her white and pink dresses. Her beautiful black shoes had become filthy. She had lost her handbag and compact. Her husband had displayed selfish and unattractive aspects which she had not believed existed in him. On the evening before they went back they had dinner in the French restaurant on the top floor of the hotel. Jamila was utterly depressed. She wept as she cut the meat. Tears started to pour on the plates in front of her. Her husband noticed that she was crying and asked her with confused concern what the matter was. She dried her eyes with a table napkin and said that the sight of the children of the family having dinner at the next table made her miss her own children.

IV

When she got home the telephone did not stop ringing. Greetings. Welcome back. Questions and enquiries about the trip to Bombay. Jamila spoke joyfully and cheerfully. She thanked each of her callers and chatted to everybody and told them in exhaustive detail about her wonderful trip to India.

'The weather was invigorating and the scent of the jasmine that children were selling was quite intoxicating.'

'The white hall of the hotel with its marble columns was just like a film set. We sat – Abu Khalifa and I – on a huge wooden swing and watched people swimming. We ate sandwiches and drank juice and some darling little cats rubbed up against our legs. We were so happy and had such a relaxing time.'

'The embroidery of the dresses and jallabiyas is simply amazing. Abu Khalifa was full of praise for my taste. He urged me to buy more and gave a huge tip to the salesman.'

'The grilled maize sold by the Gateway to India is absolutely delicious, especially when they sprinkle it with salt and squeeze a bit of lemon on it.'

'Elephanta Island with its monkeys is one of the most beautiful spots in the world. We spent there four happy hours which we'll never forget for the rest of our lives.'

'The trip was wonderful, perfectly marvellous. Ah, travel's so lovely, such a delight.'

6

Bombay or Bust

The Venerable Gentlemen

They were all venerable gentlemen. I would gaze at their beards, some white, some dyed, at their moustaches, some long, some short, at their thawbs, white, brown and light yellow, at their coats of wool and of cotton, at their gold Parker pens which they did not often use, at their teeth, some natural, some false. One or two of them had sticks with ivory hands, some had gold lighters. They had shawls of cotton and of expensive wool. The scent of sandalwood and the fragrance of perfume drifted from them. They fingered prayer beads of ivory and amber, their shoes were of bright leather and some of them had developed paunches. Even the slimness of those who were slim was not the slimness of poverty which makes the skin shrivel up and dry. It was the slimness of affluence: the skin becomes soft with something of vigour and freshness. Respectability, dignity and gravity appeared not only on their bodies and clothes and on their external forms but also in their speech and their movements.

problems of inheritance or on the law relating to the division and distribution of inherited property. Al Hajj Ahmad was the authority on this subject. He would display his knowledge and understanding of these matters to his colleagues whenever they sat together. Global and Arab politics were also among the favoured topics of discussion at their sessions. Usually they would talk about the news and comments broadcast from London. The professor of political conversation was the owner of the shop, Abu Khalid. In addition to London, he would listen in to a number of world radio stations such as Voice of America and Monte Carlo and to a handful of Arab stations as well. He was aided in this by an enormous Phillips radio with an abundance of wavelengths and by a vigorous memory which never lost track of detail or of matters of secondary importance.

I had got to know Abu Khalid about a year ago through a relation of mine who was well aware that a government salary was not enough and suggested that I work in the evening in Abu Khalid's shop and sort out his accounts and business papers. Abu Khalid had at once got rid of an Indian accountant on the grounds that he was cheating him and had built a factory in his home town in Kerala from funds he had embezzled from him. The business affairs and accounts of Abu Khalid were really quite simple. There were thirty shops and four tower blocks of varying importance and size. The basic task was to collect the rent and to pay it into Abu Khalid's account at the bank. The lessees of the shops came at different times of the year to hand over the rent and to receive the tenancy agreement. As for the blocks there was a property agency that dealt with the rents of the shops and the flats. They gave Abu Khalid one lump sum each year which relieved him from the hassle of the tenants with their complaints.

When you saw Abu Khalid's shop for the first time you would imagine that it belonged to some luckless trader. The desk and walls were of formica. There was a calendar over the leather chair where Abu Khalid sat. There was nothing to suggest opulence or ease of circumstances except those six or eight venerable gentlemen who seemed from their appearance to be exemplars of prosperity. The talk of these venerable genetlemen was not confined to matters of inheritance or to politics. They would offer their considered views on the management of local government departments. They criticised some things that had been done and discussed the latest social events without descending to rumour or trivia. Sometimes they spoke about literature or poetry. In this field it was Abu Salim who was the expert. He knew by heart a lot of poetry from the Jahiliya, from Mutanabbi and from Shawqi. Their talk was full of maturity and of authority, the harvest of their years and of the different experiences of life and of the hard times that had moulded them. In their youth they had worked as pearl fishers. Then they had travelled in different countries where they worked as small traders. They had toiled and struggled, married and brought up children and now most of them had young grand-children. I felt relaxed as I listened to their talk which left me with the positive impression that advanced years meant not just illness, physical frailty and whiteness of hair and beard but it also brought with it repose, the triumph over the vicissitudes and passions of youth, the cooling of carnal appetites. In their place was meditation upon the meaning of life and upon the aim of existence, sufi and spiritual contemplation.

When I compared them with my own friends, when I contrasted the talk of these venerable gentlemen with the chatter of mates of my own age I smiled, indeed I laughed. Although I was very fond of my friends at the coffee house, their talk was superficial and banal. It was nearly all about sport and women. There was Ubaid who had had a telephone romance for six months with some girl and when in the end he met her he discovered that she was as ugly as sin. And Ibrahim who was picked up by the police when he was in a lonely spot on the beach with a girl in his car and was able to avoid scandal for himself and for her by ramming the police car into the sand with his fast jeep. And there was Khamis the Idiot who was deeply in love with a girl and sent her many valuable presents. He finally discovered that she was married with five children. When he went to reclaim the presents the husband laughed at him and when he insisted the husband punched him in the face, knocking out one of his front teeth. How could such frivolity compare with the conversation of these venerable gentle-men. It was the difference of chalk and cheese, of heaven and earth.

The Passion of Fruit

All these venerable gentlemen including Abu Khalid used to spend several months each year in Bombay. When they returned they never wearied of talking about Bombay. Their conversation as always was measured and respectable. Much of it concentrated on the allure of the food of Bombay. The most eloquent in this respect was Abu Salim, the lover of literature and poetry.

'No place in the world compares with Bombay, for the abundance of its fruit,' he used to say. 'Everything is there in plenty. Many varieties of mango. Different kinds of bananas. The mandarins are far better than the oranges of Syria and Lebanon. There are watermelons and honeydew melons that weight several kilograms.'

Abu Salim was not content with that cool and comprehensive appraisal but launched into lyrical detail.

'The red and yellow Alfonso mango is like the cheek of a blushing young virgin when an indelicate word ruffles her composure. The aroma of slices of the fragrant watermelon are like the smell of the mouth of a young child. The touch of a yellow banana is as soft as Chinese silk. The mandarin beckons to you as you enter the fruit market. The black grapes tempt you to sample their sweetness. The chico dances before you. Peaches and pears flaunt themselves in front of your eyes with all the seductive fascination of one offering herself for you to take, to smell and to bite.'

The others agreed and each commented how right he was and would then talk of his own favourite fruit. For Abu Khalid it was mangoes. Abu Ulya would die for watermelons and Khalfan loved honeydew melons. Abu Sultan was captivated by grapes. Abu Ahmad adored chico fruit and Humaid was devoted to oranges. And it was not only fruit that attracted them to Bombay. There was also milk. Abu Khalid used to talk a lot about the milk.

'The buffaloes' milk of Bombay! I was enraptured by it over thirty years ago when I went to India for the first time. I was a slim pale young man. One month after drinking that milk I got fat and ruddy-cheeked and ever since I have been an addict. Indian buffaloes' milk is nutritious, fattening and tasty and is superior to any other kind of milk I have drunk in all my life either in Dubai or in any other city of the world I have been to.'

The others backed him up and Abu Ahmad explained that the reason for the fattening quality of buffaloes' milk was the greenness of the pasturelands of the Indian valleys.

Abu Sultan loved Indian sweets and the faluda that was made at the Padishah restaurant stall in the Orient Hotel near the central fruit and vegetable market. He spoke of faluda in the language of an infatuated lover.

Humaid too loved and lauded Indian food.

'The Indian restaurants,' he said, 'are the richest and most superb restaurants in the world. For centuries right up to the present day the rest of the world have taken from India all those gorgeous spices without which food would have no taste or attraction for anybody. In the past Europeans used to pay gold for Indian pepper. The tastiest tandoori chicken of the east that you can possibly eat is to be found in the Delhi Durbar restaurant in Bombay. And the best biryani can be found at the Gaylord restaurant in Bombay as well.'

Abu Ulya was a perfume merchant and for that reason always used to talk about the magnificent Indian perfumes.

'Real sandalwood comes from Bombay. All that sandalwood they bring in from Singapore, Thailand and Burma is inferior stuff. It smells awful and is unsuitable for respectable folk. People of refined sensibilities scoff at those without taste who cannot tell the difference between sandalwood and matchsticks.'

I asked him once about the new sandalwood perfume which they put into a big bottle with a spout.

'That is not sandalwood perfume,' he said disparagingly. 'It is some obnoxious concoction made from foul perfumes and smells given off by evil-smelling insects.'

Khalfan had another excellent reason for liking Bombay.

'In Bombay,' he said, 'I feel as if I am appreciated and respected. Shopkeepers stand up when I pass and they all say, "Come in, my Arab lord." I walk along as if I am a Sultan. In London or in other European cities they look askance at us as if we were servants. They never forget that they used until quite recently to colonise us.'

Abu Ahmad agreed with Khalfan and said, 'And language, that great stumbling block. In Bombay I can talk to anybody – in the hotel, in the shops and in taxis in Hindi. I understand what they want and they understand what I want. But if I go to London I have to take an interpreter because I don't know English.'

I had never been to Bombay but the talk of these venerable gentlemen made it seem as if I was tasting the fruit and walking through the streets, calling in at the hotels, smelling the scents and perfumes and talking with the people of Bombay. I imagined it as an oriental city with traditional bazaars and splendid buildings with fine columns and coloured domes. I asked a friend at the coffee house who had been there about Bombay. He cursed it abominably and described it as the most wretched and filthy city in the world. I took no notice of what he said. I might have expected it for he was not concerned with any matters of taste or with its picturesque aspects. He used to go to Bangkok only to indulge in his carnal appetites. The venerable gentlemen were interested in fruit, perfumes, fine food, delicious sweets, the superb architecture and other refined delights about which, then they talked, their enthusiasm never flagged.

Exposure and Revelation

One evening half an hour before the shop closed I was going over some leases. The shop was filled with the venerable gentlemen. Khalfan and Abu Sultan were talking loudly at each other.

'I have not cheated you over the sale of a plot of land,' Khalfan shouted. 'You sold it to me of your own free will. Why have you changed your mind now six months later when the price of land has gone up?'

'The price of land has gone up quite unreasonably,' Abu Sultan replied angrily. 'There's no doubt there's something fishy in it all.'

'It's an ordinary transaction of selling and buying,' Khalfan said impatiently.

'In six months you've made three million dirhams out of me,' replied Abu Sultan. 'Where's the justice in that? Where's right? Where's equity?'

'You'd already sold scores of plots.'

'Yes, but nobody exploited me like this and I have never before lost so much money.'

'Why don't you get your own back on my good luck?'

Abu Sultan then said sarcastically, 'Why did you have bad luck with Hamida?'

'What do you mean?' Khalfan exploded.

'I mean that she left you and went off to Abu Hamid who bought her a flat in a block near the President Hotel in Bombay.'

'I'm not daft like you,' Khalfan said, shaking with anger. 'Whores don't laugh at my beard. How much did you spend on that fat peasant, Samiha? On one single trip you poured half a million rupees on her. You could have bought a factory in Bombay with that money.'

'It's my money and I can do what I like with it,' Abu Sultan shouted back. 'If I want one of those girls then I will spend all the money I like on her. Are you partner in my financial affairs?'

Humaid then smiled and said, 'My word, my word. So Abu Hamid pinched Hamida from Khalfan, then.'

Khalfan turned on him. 'Shut up,' he snapped. 'Have you forgotten all about that skinny girl at whom you threw heaps of money after she made a fool of you, persuading you that she was a famous Indian film star? We learnt later that she had made her pile from working in the parlours of Faris Road.'

Abu Khalid looked towards my small desk and said quietly, 'This is not the place to talk about such things.'

Khalfan was shaking even more after the story of Hamida had been told in front of everybody. He was no longer able to control his feelings or his tongue.

'Abu Khalid now gives us the benefit of his advice,' he said. 'Why didn't you take your own advice when that Indian Christian girl Liza was leading you by the nose through the bars and night clubs of Bombay as if you were her lapdog. She used to put coloured paper streamers round your neck and a comic hat on your head at Christmas and New Year parties. And when was that crazy infatuation? Just last year. Have you forgotten?'

Abu Ulya, who was paralysed and in a wheel-chair, wanted to say something to calm things down. He wiped his white beard, played with his prayer beads and said, 'Steady on, steady on. What's it all about?'

Khalfan turned on him and said angrily, 'Now it's telling prayer beads and objecting to stories about girls, and trying to cool things. Only last summer in your room at the Taj Mahal Hotel you had three girls with you. Have you forgotten? Isn't one enough for you, you goat?'

Abu Ulya turned to Khalfan with a look of alarm on his face. He then turned to the others and gave a sign to his Sri Lankan attendant to wheel him out of the shop. He said as he was leaving, 'I brought three girls! God forbid. Khalfan's lost his wits. God forbid. What is all this talk? He should control his unruly tongue. What is all this talk?'

7
Father and Son

I

Infancy and boyhood are strange stages in the life of man. Many people, especially when they are getting on in years, look back on their childhood with affection and nostalgia and a sort of romanticism. They talk with tenderness and fascination about the games they played and of the hardships and the joys of their early days.

Isa bin Majid was not one of these. His childhood was difficult, harsh and uncertain. He cannot remember the games he played. He has no memories of a happy childhood. Indeed apart from a few images that are as rooted in his mind as the iron stakes at the side of the creek in Dubai he has forgotten most of the events of his childhood.

The first image goes back to when he was eight years old. His father used to take him from Shindagha where he worked as a muezzin and imam in one of the mosques to Deira to sit with people attending the majlises of the pearl merchants and sea captains. He would watch the buying and selling of pearls at the time when prices were sliding. The optimism of previous years was gone and the old pearls no longer retained their magic. Even the famous merchant al Hajj Muhammad bin Khalid lost his dignity and standing when he had to haggle over prices and shout at those who brought in purses of pearls. The world of relative

53

comfort was gradually falling apart. Testing times confronted many at the beginning of the forties in different parts of the world, not least in the war zones of Europe and Asia, and reached even Dubai.

One sunny winter morning in a remote corner of the dried fish market Isa was watching his father having his blood cupped. His father looked odd. The cupper's horn was placed on an exposed part of his father's head. He recalled one of his mother's tales about the two-horned devil. His father seemed to be like a devil with one horn. The horn was removed to reveal a slight swelling. The blood cupper then took a razor and slashed at the swelling with a few rapid strokes inflicting a light injury. The cupper applied the horn to the swelling again and began to suck out through the hole at the end. His eyes got redder and his cheeks became thinner. He looked very odd indeed. The horn was again removed. The swelling was covered with black blood. The cupper wiped it away and replaced the horn. The operation was repeated three or four times.

When the blood cupper had finished his work, Majid got up to go. Isa went up to his father who put his taqia and ghutra back on his head, placed his aba'a over his shoulder and tossed a coin to the cupper who looked to see how much it was and then shouted angrily that it was not enough. It was Isa's father's turn to get angry. He took the coin back, took Isa's hand and turned to walk away. The cupper got up and seized the edge of his aba'a. Majid released his son's hand and started to grapple with the cupper. He was still weak from the operation and blood was flowing from him, but he was able to prolong the struggle. The cupper took out a knife and stabbed Majid. The knife went right through the heart. Majid fell. The cupper looked around and then fled down one of the alleyways leaving behind the body, the instruments for cupping, and Isa. It all happened very quickly. Isa looked at his father who was sprawled on his back with blood staining his white thawb and aba'a. He was groaning and had his hand on his heart. After a short while he became still. Flies came and settled on the blood trickling from his head, his lips, his nose and his eyes.

Isa did not yet understand the mystery of death. He knew that something very serious had happened to his father but he could not imagine that it was the end. How could his huge strong father stop existing? The imam, the man who recited the Qur'an? He could not just die and stop reciting the Qur'an. He sat down by his father's head and swatted the flies away from his face. After a while a lot of people came up. He could not remember much more after that, but he does remember that the following morning he saw the cupper tied up near one of the mud brick towers. His eyes were wandering. He next saw three of his uncles, his aunts and some guards. He does not know who brought him to be part of the crowd gathered to witness the sentence of execution on his father's murderer, which the authorities had decreed should be in the same way that his father died. In a few fleeting moments he saw his uncles plunging their knives into the stomach, chest and face of the blood cupper who uttered two shrieks and fell.

II

The second image was when he was fifteen years old. He was afflicted by a terrible fever. His back was inflamed and his voice was so strained that he was unable to talk. He was weak and delirious. At first his mother thought that it was an ordinary fever and gave him some warm thyme juice to drink. He threw it up.

Four days later small pustules started appearing all over his body. His mother realised that he had smallpox. An uncle came and carried him to the hospice built by a philanthropist close to the Creek on the Deira side, an isolation hospice for those suffering from smallpox. In his first days in the vault-like hospice chambers he would listen to the wails and sighs of the other patients. Some were raving, others were reciting what they could remember of Qur'anic verses and prayers in feeble tones of entreaty. One of them wept day and night from fear of death that often stalked these chambers.

On his fourth day they brought in one of his childhood friends, Sulaiman. He was shocked when he saw his face. The disfigurement caused by the smallpox was hideous. In contrast to the many swarthy boys in the Shindagha area, Sulaiman was quite fair. His eyes were green because his mother had come from the Ruus al Jibal area. When they teased him the boys used to call him 'The Englishman' and 'Cat's Eyes'. He had been a bonny lad but the smallpox ravaged his face and body horribly. The hospice warden, Salim, brought him some rice but he was unable to eat it. He died the night after they brought him in. Next morning Isa looked in despair at Salim as he dragged Sulaiman's body from the adjacent chamber.

Each day his mother would send him some sugar cakes in the popular belief that sweet foods helped to bring the pustules to maturity. That day he ate four sugar cakes all at once. On his fifteenth night the fever became intense and the pustules became enormous. It was as if they were another layer of flesh that was worn on top of his own skin. That night he had the sensation of the foreboding presence of Death in the chamber. It was imminent and it was frightening. His throat was dry and his extremities felt frozen. But extraordinarily his heart did not beat more rapidly but began to slow down. He closed his eyes and offered total surrender.

Next morning the pustules began to break open. The smallpox was not going to kill him. After forty five days the period of isolation was over. Salim took him to the Creek to wash his body and face in its waters. The water was extremely calm. Isa saw his face reflected. It was a new face full of pock marks. He rejoiced at the sight of fish sporting in the water nearby.

III

In those days there were two unavoidable tasks that the quarter required of every young man of twenty. The first was to marry and the second was to father children. At the age of twenty Isa married the daughter of one of his paternal uncles. For three years there were no children.

He thought of marrying a second time but he loved his cousin and moreover lacked the means of marry again. His income was very modest. When he was young he used to help the fishermen grease their boats, spread the nets out and push the boats into the sea. They used to give him some fish most of which he was able to sell in the suq. He would bring his mother the money and the rest of the fish, just skin and bone, that he was unable to sell. At the time he got married he was a fisherman himself and used to go fishing with a group. On one occasion he complained to a friend about his wife not having any children. The friend advised him to go to the sidr tree of Sayyid Hashim. One day he was sent to buy some rope from the stall belonging to Khalifa al Suri. The stall was made of palm leaves where the owner sold everything needed for fishing like ropes, nets, grease and so on and so forth. Isa asked about the blessings to be obtained from Sayyid Hashim.

'Don't believe these fairy stories', Khalifa said as he was winding up rope in his hand, 'It's an idle legend. Whenever were trees either useful or harmful? Your sayyid if he could would have saved himself. He was killed by his slave and could not even help himself.'

Isa was not convinced by the answer given by Khalifa who was a sardonic individual who never left his stall even to pray. All he was interested in was buying and selling and the sound of cash.

Isa asked Shaikh Muhammad, an old friend of his father's, about Sayyid Hashim. In a voice full of sorrow he replied, 'I used to be a follower of the Sayyid. He was a great saint and a true believer who performed miraculous deeds. He used to commemorate sacred nights at his unblemished home. We used to assist in his performances. From the same pot held in his hands he would pour me a glass of fruit juice, a glass of sweet water and a glass of buttermilk that had the sweetness of honey. Whoever tasted these glasses would have believed that they were not the produce of this world but were from the blessings and boons of heaven above. But we were unfortunate for he did not reside long with us.'

'How was that?' asked Isa.

Shaikh Muhammad said dolefully, 'He went where it was decreed that his martyrdom would take place, at the city of Linja. He embarked upon a journey to an encounter with the Lord, an encounter for which he had longed all his life and about which he had sung anthems.'

'They say his slave killed him,' Isa said cautiously.

'Bilal was not the man to kill him', replied Shaikh Muhammad in a deep voice. 'He was his son, his slave, his friend, his pupil and his servant. He was not bold enough or capable enough to do that. The matter was put into his hands. He it was to whom was given the Isfahani knife. Bilal was carrying out a higher wish. After the deed was done, his face was, as the story-tellers say, radiant with light. In that instant ecstasy dominated all else.' He sighed. 'We were unfortunate. We were unfortunate. Nothing was left to us but this blessed tree which used to shelter that wonderful Sayyid.'

That evening Isa went with his wife to visit the sidr of Sayyid Hashim. The sight of the three trees at the setting of the sun was majestic. They brought some incense. He prayed with his wife, saying two prayers in honour of the Sayyid. A few months after the visit his wife gave birth to his only son, Rashid.

IV

The Son

Rashid, the son, whom Isa obtained from the blessings of the tree of the Sayyid, also lived a life sustained with blessings. He was a victim of all the diseases of infancy, measles, whooping cough and all manner of fevers. Most of them were severe. Each illness and fever would have killed him but for his lucky star and an Indian who was one of the few doctors in Dubai at that time. His name was difficult to pronounce and so, by common consent, the people of Dubai called him Dr Black on account of his dark complexion. Isa often used to take Rashid, even on cold winter nights, to see Dr Black who lived and had his practice in the same building. When Rashid had a very severe fever Isa would communicate his anxiety about his son's survival to Dr Black who would smile and tell him he should have no fear and that Rashid would not die in Dubai.

Rashid went to the intermediate school where he was an out-standing troublemaker. In spite of severe beatings received from his father and from his teachers he did not give up his deviant behaviour. He would always be late and one day in the daily assembly he failed to salute the flag. When his fellow-students chanted the slogan, 'Our fatherland, from the Ocean to the Gulf, our nation. One Arab Nation. We will die so that Arab nationalism can live', he would mock the words and chant slightly differently from the others. Climbing over the school walls and playing truant were regular practices. Even the Palestinian Deputy Principal, with all his nationalist fervour, despaired of his conduct.

Perhaps the strangest sight the school ever saw was when a well-known Iranian madame came up to the school. She was enormous, had a distinctive aba'a, a glittering burqu' and wide protruding eyes. She came to complain about Rashid and some of his chums who had stolen her chicken and duck from her house near the school and sold them in the suq. After that incident Rashid was absent from the school for a week. When Isa brought him to the Principal apologising for the incident, the latter would have expelled him altogether but for Isa's pleading and the Deputy's nationalist fervour.

Rashid continued to fail exams at every level over and over again to the extent that he was already seventeen years old when he reached the fourth year intermediate. His father gave up and withdrew him from the school. His father now had a medium-sized fishing boat with three sailors working for him.

Rashid got a job as collector of municipal taxes. He would go among the fishmongers, butchers and so on in order to take the municipality fees. Most of them would go into his pocket. After the Emirates became independent, Rashid set up three bogus companies for getting permission for obtaining visas for groups and for individuals. The name of the first company was 'The Black Cats' Company', the second, 'The Radiant Emirates Company' and the third 'The Big Five Company'. He used to sell a visa for 5000 dirhams. He acquired some small capital and bought for his father a large launch, much bigger than his previous boat, and insisted on calling it 'The Visa'. He went to Egypt and married an Egyptian peasant girl called Fatma. Two months later he went to India and married another girl whose name was Khadija. His father was not at all pleased with Rashid's behaviour.

After independence many of Isa's colleagues left the sea. Some went to live with their sons and others worked as servants or messengers in the Ministries and schools. Yet others lived on the income provided by the Department of Social Affairs. But Isa continued working and was sceptical about the matter of oil wealth because he had lived most of his life in toil, drudgery and hardship, having to snatch a livelihood from the cruel sea. He was not happy about the opulence which came to many without any effort or hardship. He used often to say,

'Money that comes effortlessly, doesn't last.'

It made no sense to him that even servants, fishermen and sailors now had motorcars and in their homes Indian servants.

Another strange thing was that idle people who really did not know much managed to get their hands on a lot of money. Even the Bedu were spending and squandering thousands on their sons' weddings.

V

Last summer Rashid went with some friends to Bangkok. One foggy morning Isa and his men were bringing in some fish near the fishmarket in Dubai. A policeman came up to him. He was a friend of Rashid's and told him that Rashid had been killed in a brawl in a Bangkok nightclub.

He was stunned by the news. He sat down bewildered, his eyes looking towards the waters of the Creek. It was hard to see the details of the other side because of fog. He recalled his father's corpse and his uncles as they stabbed the blood cupper to death. He recalled the sidr of Sayyid Hashim and Dr Black. He wiped his face and said, his voice quaking and sepulchral, 'We are from God and to God we shall return.'

8

Antar

There are not many people who are happy and rejoice at their father's death. Hamdan was one such person. His father had been a harsh tyrant whose idea of bringing up children was as follows: when a father is severe with his son, he ensures that the son will be tough and will consequently succeed in life. This theory did not work in Hamdan's case for he failed in his studies and did not prosper in his father's shop from which he often escaped to wander aimlessly around the labyrinthine suqs of Deira.

His father sent him to the army where he spent four months, followed by two months in prison for having struck the camp cook. Hamdan insisted that the cook had provoked him and had made improper demands.

When he heard that his father had died he was overjoyed, for he was the sole heir. He spent three days of the mourning period getting drunk in the flat of one of his mates who joined in the celebration. His father's estate, cash and property, was worth three million dirhams. In one year Hamdan spent most of that sum in the following manner: one month in Dubai, one month in Bombay, two months in Dubai, two months in Bangkok and Pataya . . . and so on. On each of these trips Hamdan would take with him a group of young friends – never less than four at one time – and they would all eat, drink and enjoy themselves at Hamdan's expense, for he savoured the new sensation of wealth and precedence. These young men would cheer Hamdan on, with expressions like 'Long life to you', 'At your service', 'We're all yours'. When he wanted to get into a taxi one of them would run to open the door for him with respectful deference. When he took out a cigarette to smoke, two of them would argue as to which of them would be lucky enough to have the honour of lighting that cigarette. When he bought something or other from those suqs of Asia, the parasite friends would insist on carrying his bags however light they were so as to spare Hamdan any trouble. And when some drunkard in a night club picked a quarrel with Hamdan the lads would be quick to sort him out and beat him up.

II

In Dubai Hamdan rented a big flat in one of the new buildings where he would sit up every night till dawn with never less than ten others. At the end of the year the reduction in his inheritance led to a reduction in his luxuries and expenses. There were fewer trips abroad. He had been accustomed at first to bring along European girls and air hostesses from the foreign airlines to join him in fun and games all night. He then had Ethiopian girls, then Indian girls and after that there was no female presence at the flat at all. At first he had been accustomed, with his friends, to dine on a whole sheep every night. Then the servants cooked only three kilograms of meat and after that they were reduced to one frozen chicken. Finally they were down to shawarma and falafil sand-wiches, which the Indian servant brought in from a nearby restau-rant. Drink was also affected. At first it was the best brand of whisky, gin, vodka and beer. At the end of the night some of the lads would take as they left half bottles of whisky and indeed some that were almost full. Then the parties were cut down to two bottles of whisky and the iced cans of beer disappeared altogether. In the end Hamdan was obliged to say sorrowfully to his friends, whose number had declined with the decline in circumstances, that anyone who wanted to have a drink in his flat would have to bring his drink with him. Perhaps the strangest episode in Ham-dan's story is about the lion.

III

In the middle of the year of prosperity Hamdan heard from one of the lads in the flat that there was a firm in Holland that was able to export to any part of the world whatever rare animal was required. Hamdan was shown a catalogue that had in it coloured pictures of different animals. He saw pictures of gorillas, of turtles, of cheetahs – the fastest animals in the world – of tigers and snakes . . . and so on. He paused at the picture of the lion. He examined it closely. Since he was small he had been fascinated by this obscure, ferocious, huge beast, the king of the jungle. As long as he had the money he inherited from his father he felt he was in every way a king except for the crown. Why should he not purchase a lion? He liked the idea. He was not bothered by the high price, although he was anxious about the animal's fierce reputation. One friend assured him, saying that this lion would have been brought up since it was a cub in the company's zoo and would be more or less tame. He put in an order for the lion and paid 100,000 dirhams. The actual price with the cost of freight was 60,000 dirhams. The remaining 40,000 dirhams went into the pocket of one of his mates as commission for the great efforts he had taken to send the letter and money order to the aforesaid company in Amsterdam.

When the lion arrived Hamdan put it in one of the three bedrooms of the flat used for amusement. His friends of the nightly revels were taken aback. They were alarmed and very worried when they saw it. Some of them jumped out through the window. Others hid themselves behind the armchairs. Hamdan held an iron chain round the lion's neck and laughed at his scared friends. After a while they became used to it and took to playing with it until they got bored. Hamdan gave it the name Antar. One day he took it to his old aunt who was frightened out of her wits at the sight and cursed her depraved nephew whose only occupation was looking after animals and other strange things. In the early days he would go for rides with Antar in his American car and take him for walks in the streets of Dubai. He would derive enormous pleasure from seeing people in other cars and on the pavements pointing to his car and to his lion, Antar, sitting beside him.

IV

Four months after acquiring Antar, Hamdan began to worry about it, especially as the money from his father's inheritance was running out. Hamdan had never in all his life seen an animal with such an appetite. In one day he would buy for it three kilos of meat. Then he was forced to buy instead four chickens. Eventually his financial problems increased and he was no longer able to afford to keep Antar, so he decided to try to get rid of it. He thought of his Uncle Salman, a businessman, with a good income derived from property. He had not seen him for ten years. He went to call at his fine quiet house, the paved area outside and the floor of the reception room all of coloured marble. It reminded him of the superbly build Chinese cemeteries that he had seen in Manila. The uncle was not pleased when he turned up because he had loathed Hamdan's father and had heard quite enough of Hamdan's extravagance, but duty obliged him to receive him. When he announced that he wanted to make a present of the lion, Antar, his uncle sent him packing without further ado. Hamdan was upset and returned to the flat. Antar was still consuming four chickens a day.

He went to see his old neighbour, Hajj Abu Salim, who had become very rich after a number of deals with the government. He said in amazement, 'What, you want to give me a lion?'

'Yes, uncle Abu Salim.'

He was even more taken aback. 'What am I going to do with it?'

'The children will be amused by it.'

'My children will be amused by a lion? Have you gone mad?'

'No, uncle Abu Salim. It's quite tame and can live with you in the house or you can take it to the farm at Khawanij.'

When he left, Hajj Abu Salim got in touch with Hamdan's uncle, 'I've heard that your nephew was a bit boisterous but I had not heard that he'd gone mad.'

'What's he done?'

'He wants to give me a lion.'

Hamdan went back to the flat. Antar was still hungry. He thought for a little while. Why not offer it to the zoo? They would be delighted with it and would want no return. They would relieve him of the expense. He would be able to come from time to time and look at it and stroke it. He went to the zoo to talk about the matter. The man in charge took off his glasses, folded his hands and placed them on the files that were piled high on his desk, thought for a moment and then said, 'Listen, Mr Hamdan. I wish to be quite frank with you. Our expenses are huge and we do not have many visitors. We do not bring in any new animals. If you want us to keep the lion you must at your own expense have a cage constructed of cement and steel. You will have to pay us the cost of feeding it on a monthly basis. These are the conditions for our looking after the lion for you.'

V

Hamdan went back and drank half a bottle of vodka. He was cross and utterly fed up. He took a revolver and shot Antar through the head five times. Antar turned over on its right side. Drops of blood poured out. With the help of his servant he carried it out to the car and took it to the slaughterhouse in the meat market. They skinned it for fifty dirhams . . . Hamdan still kept Antar's hide in the car though.

9
'Your Uncle Was a Poet'

'Your uncle was a poet.'

Khalifa's mother did not know that the words she uttered would have such an impact on her son. She was having dinner with him and they were watching television. A programme had started about Nabati poetry. She was talking to her son about the divorce of a neighbour's daughter and then suddenly said, prompted by something on the television, 'Your uncle was a poet'.

That sentence stuck in Khalifa's mind. There was earlier poetic talent in the family.

Khalifa was a young junior official and read lots of magazines and newspapers. He knew that plenty of things were due to heredity. His voice, for example, was high like that of his mother's brother. His father was bald and here he was, his hair beginning to recede. His eyes were grey like those of his mother. Talent was also heredity. His uncle was a poet. There was no doubt that in the family there would be people who were ready to recite poetry. When he went that night to a neighbour's house he lost terribly at rummy, even though he was a master of the game. His mother's sentence went dancing through his brain making it impossible for him to concentrate.

'Your uncle was a poet.'

He was only able to lay his hands on two poems said to have been written by his uncle. He started to read all the Nabati poetry

67

pages in the Emirates and Gulf newspapers.

'Your uncle was a poet.'

Yes, he could become a poet like his uncle. The talent ran in the family. His friend, Jasim, dropped by. He had just bought a new Japanese car and wanted to celebrate with him. Jasim had half a carton of beer. They went to the beach. Khalifa drank three cans. He was not listening to Jasim's chatter about the specifications of his new car. He was gazing at the sunset, absorbed in its fascination.

'Your uncle was a poet.'

At nine that evening Jasim brought him home. He told his mother that he had already eaten. He shut himself up in his room and took from the wardrobe some notepaper. The pages were pink and each page had a border of coloured hearts. He began to write. Four hours went by. At exactly one o'clock in the morning he finished, tired and happy at the same time. He had written his first poem with thirty verses. A love poem. Poems with a moral and poems with riddles would have their turns in the future. He had to start with a poem of love.

II

Next morning Khalifa went to see his friend, Muhammad, the secretary to the man in charge of the department he worked in. He asked him to type out the verses. His own handwriting was very untidy and the people at the newspaper to whom he was going to send his poem would not be able to read it. The secretary did not understand poetry, or anything else, but agreed. The only hobby in which his feelings and interest were engaged was fishing. Khalifa looked at the typed poem and was at first quite pleased. Then he remembered that one of his colleagues in the Department of Financial Affairs, the Egyptian, Sami, was an excellent calligrapher. He took the poem to him to write out in his beautiful hand. Sami read it and burst out laughing, 'What's this rubbish?'

Khalifa said, indignantly, 'My dear chap, all I want is a simple service from you. There's no need for such remarks. Anyway you don't know anything about Nabati poetry.'

Sami wrote it out for him in the ruq'a script. It looked really beautiful. Khalifa put it in a pretty envelope and typed the newspaper's address on it. He did not trust the department's messenger. He took it along himself to the central post office which was near the department's building.

III

After he sent his poem to the newspaper to publish on the Nabati poetry page, his heart was full of expectation. The editor of the page was sure to like it and find it amazing. He would certainly know that his uncle was a poet and that the poetic talent ran in the family. Where would they publish it? At the top of the page, of course. Or in the middle with a picture of a beautiful Bedu girl or of gazelles. Gazelles would be better. Without any doubt one of the well-known entertainers would like it and sing it. 'And after that other poets will write poems of criticism. Of course they'll want to criticise me and I'll reply to them and blacken their reputations. People will say, "Have you heard and read the reply of Khalifa, the famous poet, to the poem of So-and-so or Such-and-such?" And the girls, how could I forget about them? After my poems are published, lovely girls will pester me by phone. I'll have to write to the telephone exchange. "The girl who is asking for me and refuses to give you her name. Don't transfer her call to me. Say I'm not in. I cannot waste time talking on the phone. Any girl who wants me must come and see me." And radio and TV. "I don't like appearing on the television screen. It's true my mum says I'm the best-looking boy in the quarter, but I know she's exaggerating somewhat."

'The radio's OK, so long as the programmes are only about poetry and are broadcast at midnight. Lots of girls listen to the radio last thing at night. After a little while I'll have to publish a collection of my poems on glossy paper, of course, with coloured pictures. Cassettes of my poems could be distributed with the books, sung by one of the best-known artistes.' He thought of his mother with affection. He owed it all to her wonderful sentence.

'Your uncle was a poet.'

69

IV

In the first week the poem did not appear. There was of course a delay in the post. A letter from London to Dubai took four days. A letter from Dubai to Dubai could take over ten days. A strange business. The next week also there was nothing. Khalifa got very angry with the post. In the third week the following appeared on the page of Nabati poetry in a corner of short messages from the editor: 'To Khalifa Muhammad. Your poem is feeble in content and flawed in its metre. It is a long way from Nabati poetry but we would like to praise you for your beautiful handwriting.'

10
One Day a Week

I

Aisha alone among her friends failed to pass the secondary school certificate. She got a second grade in philosophy, a subject she hated. One week after the results came out her mother spoke seriously to her about Ali who had sought an engagement. She quickly and automatically gave her consent, out of spite for philosophy and to cock a snook at Socrates, Plato, Aristotle and al Kindi.

The first picture of Ali she saw was in the sports page of one of the daily newspapers. He had some position in one of the sports clubs. He had wide eyes, a well-trimmed moustache and beard and a short nose. She was delighted with the many presents his family bought her – jewels, gold, a valuable watch, three suitcases full of clothes, perfume and soap. They even bought her some blankets. After these presents Aisha appreciated the beard and the short nose. She cut his picture out of the paper and stuck it on to the mirror of the wardrobe that filled up her small bedroom. The wedding party, the guests, the singers. It all passed with surprising speed. Ali was very tall and did not know how to wear a bisht. He always seemed to be wearing one for the first time. As well as a beard and a small nose he also had grey eyes. Aisha was smiling all through the wedding party, in disregard of the advice given to her by her mother who told her not to smile too much in case people said she was frivolous. Two days later he took her to his house in Rashidiya.

Ali would spend six days a week in Abu Dhabi where he worked in one of the Federal Ministries. He returned on Thursday evenings and went back to Abu Dhabi on Friday afternoon. She remained in Dubai. He would phone her once or twice while he was in Abu Dhabi. In spite of these difficulties she loved him calmly at first and with a kind of contentment. Then gradually her love for Ali turned into a torrential passion. Five days a week she passed in a torment of anticipation. In the morning she would go to call on her sister who lived in the same quarter. In the afternoon she would visit her mother or go shopping. Every night before she went to sleep she would call to mind the beard, the short nose and the grey eyes. When Ali arrived on Thursday evening he was exhausted. He would have a shower and change his clothes. She would bring him a dinner that was more like a feast. Three kinds of meat, four kinds of sweet and three kinds of salad. All week she would be at work in her kitchen, preparing meals for Thursday and Friday. After dinner Ali would sit in the lounge reading newspapers, magazines and official reports.

The television would be on with the volume off. Aisha would sit on a chair opposite him. She would look at her husband as he read. Occasionally he would say something to her. She would gaze at him with devotion, looking at his eyebrows which would arch as an indication that he was reading something of importance. She felt at ease as she watched the features of his face when they were relaxed. She often went out with him after midnight for a ride in the car. He would drive in the quiet of the night from Rashidiya to al Awir, then to Khawanij – long, dark roads, sometimes lit up by the light of the moon. After that they would go to the airport at one in the morning. There he would park the car at the lower carpark and they would go to the airport cafeteria. He would order a coffee for himself and an orange-juice for her. They would stare at the passengers and at the aeroplanes as they touched down or took off. He never – not once – suggested a trip abroad. He did not even take her to Abu Dhabi. Lots of passengers carried cases and bags. Some were illiterate and gave Ali their departure cards for him to fill in. He grumbled about this job but he would be embarrassed to refuse and would do it while Aisha looked on happily. When they got home at three in the morning they would be overcome by a gentle drowsiness. Aisha's sweet weekly dream which placed her on top of the world would begin. Next morning Aisha would be up at seven. She got breakfast ready for her husband, cheese, tomatoes and milk. She would take the breakfast into the bedroom and sit down on the armchair facing the bed and do some needlework as she gazed at Ali asleep, watching him as he turned over. She would not disturb him or wake him up. She let him sleep until he woke up at ten or half past. When he had had breakfast, he would go to the garden and prune trees. He would return to watch a film on television, at the start of the day's transmissions. When he said goodbye at five and his car disappeared from sight, she wept. Not once could she prevent her eyes from filling with tears after this weekly separation.

II

One of her friends said to her as a joke, 'One day a week. What kind of a marriage is that?' Aisha was furious, dropped her friend and never spoke to her again.

III

On one occasion Ali got a bad dose of influenza. Aisha was alarmed. She took him to the doctor. When they came home she stayed up with him and was in tears all night as she watched him sweating and turning over restlessly. In the morning when he opened his eyes and smiled weakly she was overjoyed. She took his right hand and smothered it with kisses.

IV

She could not believe it when her father told her that Ali had divorced her. Even now five years after the event she still cannot accept the fact that she has been divorced by him.

11
An Icy Marriage

What a boring road

The road from Ahmad's family house in Hamriya to his new flat in a side street in the Tourist Club area of Abu Dhabi was very long. His Japanese car covered the distance in an hour and forty five minutes. Twice a week he would make the journey, first early on Saturday morning when he took his wife from the Hamriya house to Abu Dhabi and then on Thursday afternoon when he brought her back.

Throughout these two weekly journeys Ahmad would try to engage his wife in conversation about anything, but she rarely responded. He tried to interest her in all sorts of things, such as the long road, how dull and tedious it was. There were no trees at the side, no houses, no encampments, just a few squalid cafés run by feeble Malabar Indians who seemed to be suffering from tuberculosis. And the food and drink they sold seemed to have been bought when no longer fit for human consumption. His wife took no interest. Generally they took with them some fruit and bottles of mineral water. He told her that when he was studying in Britain (he had been sent by the Department to attend a three month course in accountancy the year before he got married) and went from one city to another the roads seemed to vie with one another in making things attractive for travellers. There were hills and trees, clean cafés, fine restaurants. What pleasant roads they were compared with this one which was like a desert snake with its

75

tail in Dubai and which disgorged its venom in Abu Dhabi and along whose stomach every day passed thousands of vehicles bearing tens of thousands of human beings with their petty concerns. His wife nodded in agreement. While he talked she would stare at the unending yellow desert which hugged the sea on one side and the sky on the other. She said nothing, never made any comment.

Sometimes Ahmad would make some remark on the cars that went by. Look, he's a junior official driving his car as if it is a rocket, so he can get there before his boss and so avoid a ticking off. There's a married couple who look as if they've just been quarrelling. That fellow's a senior Federal civil servant. Just look at the dumb fool. He wears his bisht even when he's driving. Before Federation he used to be a messenger in the most insignificant of departments. Now thanks to a relation who has a lot of influence in the capital he has become a very important director and is interviewed on the radio and television, using phrases like 'In actual fact', 'From an objective point of view', 'the citizens of the country', 'cadres' . . . He has no idea what they mean.

Through his work as an accountant and his many friendships Ahmad knew many of the capital's secrets and on these journeys used to gossip to his wife about the rumours and administrative feuds, about major embezzlements, bribes, scandals of foreign experts and the collapse of financial houses, about profligacy and waste, shady deals and suspicious brokers. His wife nodded in agreement and went on staring at the desert. He could not work out the mystery of her silence and her conversational inertia. At home she would chat affectionately and without inhibition with her mother and sisters, and sometimes when she was visited by the wives of friends of his in Abu Dhabi she could not stop talking. But with him she was silent, noncommittal, cold and reserved. Nothing seemed to rouse her.

Early one Saturday morning in the summer there was a thick fog on the road and they were unable to drive very fast. At the Jabal Ali roundabout they saw a frightful road accident. There was a pile-up involving ten cars. The police had arrived on the scene at once. Ahmad stopped the car and got down to see what had happened. It was an ugly sight. There was blood all over the road, and limbs of the injured spattered on the cars. Four dead bodies were laid out by the side of the road near the police car. Smashed heads and severed hands. Ahmad could stand no more of this bloody sight. He went back to the car and told his wife all about it in detail. She showed no emotion. Ten minutes later he felt dizzy. He stopped the car at the side of the road and was sick. His wife mopped his face with a small flannel and gave him some water to drink. But with him she displayed no emotion. At home when her little sister had cut her hand she had been most upset and had run about like a lunatic getting medicine and bandages. But with him she was unconcerned and unaffected.

The Absurd old Englishwoman

In their flat she carried out all her domestic duties in an exemplary manner: preparing three meals a day, usually hot meals, unlike the wives of many of his friends. She never telephoned him at the office with the classic request, 'When you come back, do drop by the take-away and bring back some food.' Whenever he returned to the flat he would find her sitting in an armchair in the reception room and in her hand an Agatha Christie detective story. She had dozens of books by that absurd old Englishwoman. He brought her volumes of the poetry of Nizar Qabbani and Mahmoud Darwish, the novels and stories of Naguib Mahfouz and Yusuf Idris. But she never opened them, not one. She persisted in her loyalty to the absurd old Englishwoman. Perhaps her loneliness was one of the reasons for her taciturnity. He tried to get her diverted. When a pet shop and nursery opened in the next block he bought her a huge Siamese cat for one thousand dirhams. She did not get very excited about it. She fed it and cleaned its quarters but did not cuddle it, tease it or even talk to it. Ahmad would bring it to the bed, stroke it and play with it. The cat purred and sharpened its claws on the bed clothes and sometimes ripped them. His wife showed no interest in the matter and made no comment. He brought her half a dozen canaries that had come from the Equatorial jungle. Again she showed no interest in them. She never mentioned them until two months later when she told him that one of them had died.

The Old Trick

In Abu Dhabi they would call on some friends. Most of their circle consisted of recently married young people from Dubai and the northern Emirates. One evening they had dinner with Ahmad's colleague, Jum'a. Ahmad was enjoying the company of Jum'a's wife. She was sympathetic and chatted away with charm and an unmalicious wit. She reminded him of an aunt of his. Jum'a's brother, Salim, was also present. He was a handsome young bachelor who had graduated from an American university. Ahmad did not like him and thought he was stuck-up. He spiced his conversation with English words and expressions quite unneces- sarily. For a long time Salim gazed at his wife and complimented her on her dress sense and how her combination of colours in what she was wearing indicated a sophisticated taste. His wife would smile at all this. Salim was the only person to whom she spoke at any length. Ahmad pondered. It was true that he had married her in the traditional way. Indeed it was almost a caricature of tradition. His aunt had chosen her for him. But she would not be unfaithful.

When they moved to the dinner table all he he could hear was the lengthy comment of Jum'a's wife about how she could not find in her local supermarket the fresh hot Indian mangos that she loved. Disturbing thoughts about his wife and Salim built up in his mind. It was the eternal triangle: an unheeding husband, a handsome boyfriend, a faithless wife. So this then accounted for her silence, her indifference and her reserve, her nodding and her lack of any interest in scandals, in death, in the cat, in the canaries. He thought carefully about how to expose the handsome boyfriend and his faithless wife. There was only one way. The husband had to be absent and the wife inviting. The lover would then come. Criminal scandal. The husband could turn up and catch the guilty couple unawares.

A week later Ahmad left the flat at five one evening, telling his wife that his Director had asked him and Jum'a to hurry up and complete the department's budget. They would spend the first part of the evening at the office and then take papers to Jum'a's flat where they would stay up until they had finished it. He would stay the night there and Juma'a's wife would go to spend the night with her people. He told her to be sure to lock the front door.

He left the flat and went to the Tourist Club. There he played ten games of billiards with another colleague who was a billiards fanatic and made the billiards room at the club his second home. Ahmad was routed in each of the ten games. He realised that he was only an average player, even below average and that his colleague was rarely defeated even when he played with the best of players. Ahmad however lost any sense of sportsmanship. He felt very cross with the result and hated this man who was trouncing him. He wished he would have a road accident and smash up his hands and be incapable of playing for the rest of his life. He left the club and walked alone on the Corniche. The sea was calm and gloomy. He watched some foreigners jogging. Crazy in this heat! People could hardly walk, let alone run. He walked from the Sheraton Hotel to the Hilton Hotel and back again. He was exhausted. He imagined the couple, absorbed in a passionate telephone conversation arranging a rendezvous. Damn the traditional marriage. She was sure to have been quite familiar with love chats over the phone before she was married. His aunt had reported that she was a poor girl who all her life had never, not once, gone out shopping. Why bother to go shopping when you had the telephone?

He dropped in on the flat of a bachelor colleague and drank three cans of beer. He did not get drunk. There were eight friends in the flat, all drinking and talking and eating. The airconditioning was not working. Ahmad looked out of the flat window that overlooked the central bus station. He saw one of the buses stop and let down five passengers. How quiet this district was at night in contrast to the din during the day. Even the pavements were having a respite from the discordant bustle of people and vehicles. He looked at his watch. A quarter to eleven. He prepared for the assault. He thought hard on the way to the flat. What would he do? Would he beat them up? Would he shout abuse at them? Would he divorce her without any further ado? When he gently opened the front door the lights of the flat were still on. He went quickly to the bedroom. The television was on though the sound was off. His wife was curled up with one of the stories of the absurd old Englishwoman. Ahmad was a little taken aback and then stammered that he and Jum'a had finished the budget in record time and so had come home. She evinced no surprise. She nodded and went off to have a glass of water. This coolness was killing him, it was so chilling.

A Late Honeymoon

When they had got married he had brought her straight to Abu Dhabi. He did not take her on a honeymoon and they never spoke about the subject. Four months after they had got married he thought that a late honeymoon would help to warm up their chilly relationship. He got tickets at a big discount through a relation who owned a small travel agency. He chose Greece about which he knew nothing in particular except that it was the home of ancient philosophy and of Aristotle Onassis who had married Jacqueline Kennedy and that Greek food was like Lebanese food. He had been impressed by the Olympic Airways publicity which showed pictures of a smiling young couple from the Gulf, happily feeding pigeons by some ancient Greek ruins. When he told his wife she did not exactly jump for joy, nor did she shower him with questions about the proposed trip. She did not even smile. All she did was nod in agreement.

They took three large suitcases with them and stayed at a small hotel near Parliament Square in Athens. They went with a tourist guide to the top of the Acropolis. The guide told them that the great architectural gem, the Parthenon, had been largely destroyed because the Turks when they had occupied Greece had used the temple as an arms store. Ahmad was not convinced by this explanation for he knew that the Greeks had no love for the Turks and were currently in dispute over Cyprus. Anyway, what was so wonderful about these absurd columns lying on the ground?

Next day his wife went down with a nasty bout of flu. She spent most of the time in bed reading more stories of the absurd old Englishwoman which she had brought along. Ahmad hated his wife's illness. Perhaps she was ill on purpose so that the trip would be a failure. He hated Greek ruins. He hated the hotel food and the tikka meat chops that were so big and tough that they needed teeth of iron to chew and digest. He hated the cold weather. It was December. A week later they were back in Abu Dhabi.

Happy Ending

Ahmad could no longer tolerate his wife's glassy cold eternally noncommittal face. He told her six months after they had been married that it could not go on and that it was better for them both to be divorced. She offered no resistance, she sought no explanation, she showed no sadness. She just looked at him in the same old way. She nodded in agreement and went off to pack her things into four large trunks.

12
A Small Ad in the Newspaper

I

Rawnaq Ali was sitting in the main mosque at Satwa listening to the Friday sermon. All he understood of it were the words, Allah, Muhammad, the Prophet, Umar and Abu Bakr. He made no sense of anything else. Ten years had passed since he came from Pakistan to Dubai. He watched films in Hindustani and listened to songs in his native Panjabi. Most of the nationals and other Arabs addressed him in Urdu. The number of words he could speak in Arabic could be counted on the fingers of his hands. He looked at a small Pathan boy sitting beside his father near one of the mosque pillars. The boy cannot have been more than seven or eight. He had his back against the pillar and had taken off his red embroidered skullcap and was playing with it, staring at the patterns and then putting it on again. He would puff up his cheeks and blow them out. Then he cracked the joints of his fingers and toes. Rawnaq wished he was a small boy like him, one who knew nothing of crime, problems or sin.

After a while Hajji Mansur came in with one of his henchmen and stood to offer two prayers of salutation to the mosque, near where Rawnaq was sitting. Rawnaq's heart beat faster. He had requested a meeting with Hajji Mansur to tell him that he had made up his mind not to work with him any more delivering hashish. He had intimated as much to Hajji Mansur's assistant when he had asked him to fix an appointment. For eight years he

83

had worked for Hajji Mansur. The police had never held him. But for the last two months and especially since his friend Aziz had committed suicide he had become very frightened. He saw the shadow of a policeman at every street corner and detected the features of an informer in the face of every customer. He did not know why Aziz had committed suicide. He had been very fond of him. He enjoyed his conversation, his jokes and witticisms and his eyes that were deep blue like crystal. Aziz used to bring him hashish and opium. Since Aziz's suicide he had had bad dreams most nights and even during afternoon naps. Sometimes he saw Aziz's head, cut off and rolling down the street, and sometimes he saw him hanging in his room, the blood trickling from his eyes, nose and mouth.

When the Friday prayers were over he left the mosque and got into a taxi driven by one of Hajji Mansur's henchmen. The car set off through the streets of Satwa towards the Trade Centre roundabout. Hajji Mansur was sitting in front by the driver. He turned to Rawnaq who was sitting in the back next to one of his men.

'They say you want to leave us,' he said loudly and deliberately.

'I . . . I . . .', stammered Rawnaq.

Hajji Mansur looked at him. His broad face was filled with anger. His beard shook as he spoke.

'What's up with you, man. Speak up.'

'I'm tired, Sir.'

Hajji Mansur laughed and said sarcastically, 'You've become tired of our work . . . Ha! ha! ha! When was our work ever tiring? You're not exactly carrying wood on your head or stones on your back.'

'But, Sir.'

'But what? Have you forgotten when you came to see me at the Aisha restaurant in the Qadir hotel in your filthy stinking rags with your body a bag of bones, out of work, without a passport and with no official papers? You didn't know how to go about doing any work. Did I not feed you?'

'Well, yes.'

'Did I not find suitable accommodation for you?'

'Yes.'

'Did I not teach you how to drive?'

'Yes.'

'Did I not get you a passport?'

'Yes.'

'Did I not find you a sponsor who got you a residence visa and all the necessary documentation?'

'Yes.'

The car passed by the Trade Centre and went off on the desert road towards Al Awir. Hajji Mansur opened the car window and spat out. He turned back to Rawnaq.

'This women in whose car you work, does she annoy you? If she doesn't please you we can find you another taxi and another sponsor.'

'No, Sir. Fatma Hasan who owns the taxi is a good woman, an excellent lady.'

'What district do you deliver in?'

'Shindagha.'

'If you don't like it I can transfer you to Qusais or Ber Dubai or to a district inside Deira.'

'I am grateful to you for your generosity, Sir, but the work doesn't suit me any more.'

Hajji Mansur became angry.

'Good God, the work doesn't suit you', he shouted. 'You've got above yourself. Three thousand dirhams from the taxi and six or seven thousand dirhams from me, that is, ten thousand a month, an income undreamt of by your father or any of your ancestors. You wretch, you waster, you dog. My God, you've got above yourself. Before you worked for me you used to sleep on a mat with that idiot Aziz. And now a room, a fine bed, a radio and cassette player, a TV and video.'

'But, Sir.'

'Shut up, you wretch. Where do you get all these things from? How did you lay your hands on them? It's thanks to me. Me. Thanks to Hajji Mansur. And now you want to leave me. You want to betray me. You want to strike the hand that has fed and clothed you, taught you and made a man of you.'

'But, Sir.'

'Silence, worm. Have you forgotten how you came to me in tears imploring me to protect your brother who had killed some-body in Lahore? We paid 50,000 rupees to the family of the murdered man so that they would leave you alone. Have you forgotten everything? Have you forgotten the favours? Have you forgotten our acts of charity?'

'I have not forgotten them, Sir. I am eternally grateful to you for your kindness.'

'If that's the case, then why do you want to leave us? Do you want to get married? I can send you to Pakistan to get married.'

For the first time the driver laughed and observed, 'Rawnaq isn't one for the women, Sir.'

Hajji Mansur ignored the driver's remark and went on, 'What do you want then? Do you want more trouble? To move about more, to deliver more so you can get more money? Our cash doesn't come from petrol. It comes from hard work. Deliver more and you can get more money.'

The car reached the end of the Awir road. The driver turned to go to Khawanij. The road was obstructed by a group of camels. Hajji Mansur looked into Rawnaq's face, 'You're stupid like these camels,' he said. 'You don't know where your interests lie.'

Rawnaq replied nervously but resolutely, 'I'm grateful to you for your kindness, Sir, but I am determined to leave.'

Hajji Mansur took out a huge handkerchief and mopped the sweat from his brow. For a long time there was silence. When they reached the Rashidiya residential area Hajji Mansur said slowly, 'If that's your last word then you are free.'

He then turned to the driver and said, 'Let's go to the garage so we can finish up Rawnaq's business and settle his account.'

Rawnaq felt easier. He had mistrusted Hajji Mansur. He would now take his money and when they parted company he would remain loyal to the memory of his service with Hajji Mansur. To the memory of Aziz and happy former days, to the memory of a life of fear, courage, terror and audacity. The car turned into a made-up side road and then on to a long sandy track. They reached the garage. A guard opened the gates into the compound. The car went by stacks of iron and various parts of old car engines. The place inspired apprehension. When they reached the big garage building they heard Indian songs coming from a tape recorder. They got out of the car and went into the huge rooms that were to the right of the garage. There they saw two of Hajji Mansur's men. They went into one room. One man closed the door. Rawnaq felt a tremor of fear. In the middle of the room he saw a huge covered plastic cistern raised on some wooden blocks. He was brought some tea. He took a sip and watched liquid dripping from the cistern on to the ground. The drips produced bubbles in the sand. Hajji Mansur spoke, loudly, harshly. 'Drink up, Rawnaq. It's the last thing you'll drink in this world.'

Rawnaq was terrified at these words and watched the acid dripping from the cistern and corroding parts of the floor. He suddenly became aware of what was in store. Panic seized him. He fell to his knees, throwing himself in front of Hajji Mansur, kissing his hand and sobbing, 'In the name of the Prophet whose tomb you have visited, spare me this fate. In the name of Ali and Fatma, of Hasan and Husain, of Abu Bakr and Umar and of all the Companions of the Prophet, spare me this death.'

Hajji Mansur withdrew his hand roughly and spat on to the floor. Two men took hold of Rawnaq who was shouting and sobbing, 'In the name of the Qur'an, I will carry on working for you. I will not leave you. I will not leave you.'

Hajji Mansur left the room and closed the door behind him.

II

One week later the following ad appeared in one of the local newspapers: 'Fatma Hasan announces that the Pakistani driver, Rawnaq Ali, who worked under her sponsorship has abandoned her service. Whoever finds him should hand him over to the nearest police station.'

13
A One-off Encounter

Khalfan had not been at all happy about his son's wish to marry that girl from Abu Dhabi. He had promised his sister that his son would marry her daughter but he gave in to his son's insistence and dogged determination. He was after all his youngest son and was financially independent. He had no power to influence him or to apply any pressure on him. He went with his son to Abu Dhabi to complete the marriage arrangements and to attend the wedding party. This was the first time he had visited Abu Dhabi. He was amazed at the extent of construction and asked his son, 'Does your bride's family live in one of these tower blocks?'

'No. They live in an ordinary house. But when we get married we shall live in a flat in one of the blocks.'

'Where do the children of these flats play and run around?'

'They are taken to the public parks.'

'Aren't these tower blocks dangerous for children? Can't they fall out of the windows?'

The son smiled and said, 'Most people in the whole world nowadays live in blocks of flats.'

Khalfan did not feel reassured by these words. They reached the bride's house. Her family greeted them. Kisses. Incense. Coffee. Rose water. Perfume. They concluded the marriage agreement. Khalfan then went with his son and some of the bride's men relatives to the Sheraton Hotel. In the hotel he stood at his son's side to receive the guests. He was a bit on edge for it was the first time he had worn the bisht. He shook hands with scores of people he did not know. He smiled and felt happier when he shook the hands of some of the friends of his son whom he had known and who had come up from Dubai to congratulate them. Before all the guests had been greeted Khalfan felt tired and withdrew into the hall. He sat down at a table. After a while a short fat man wearing a bisht with a lot of decoration came over and sat next to him. The fat man said, 'My son is a friend of the bridegroom but I don't even know the name of this bridegroom. It's become a very strange world. Are you from Dubai?'

Khalfan looked at the man and said, 'Yes. I'm from Dubai.'

The man gazed at Khalfan's face and began to stare at a scar made by branding between his eyes. He grinned broadly, got up and suddenly gave Khalfan a big hug.

'It's Khalfan, my friend from Kuwait. Al Fuhaihil. The nail. How are you, my dear friend?'

It suddenly all came back to Khalfan who said with surprise and delight, 'Rashid. Rashid Abdullah. How are you?'

As they exchanged greetings Khalfan was overcome with affection. He said, 'You still remember the story of the nail?'

'How can I ever forget it? You saved my life with the advice you gave.'

Khalfan recalled the incident. There were six migrant workers from the Emirates working in Kuwait as labourers and messengers and drivers. They all lived in one house. Four were from Dubai including Khalfan. Rashid was from Abu Dhabi and there was a sixth man from Ajman. In 1958 Rashid had bought a portrait of President Jamal Abdul Nasser whom he worshipped and whose speeches fired him with enthusiasm. He wanted to hang the picture up on the wall of the room he shared with Khalfan and the man from Ajman. He had two nails in his mouth, his hammer in his right hand and was trying to climb on to a small chair. He fell off the chair and swallowed one of the nails. He was terrified and panicked. Khalfan told him to swallow some cotton wool. He started at once to tear one of the pillows to pieces and they gave the cotton wool inside to Rashid to eat. Panic stricken Rashid swallowed a huge amount of cotton wool. Two days later Rashid relieved himself of the nail and the cotton wool.

The two men sat and talked about old times in Kuwait together. Khalfan had spent six years there from the beginning of 1957 to the end of 1962. Rashid was there for ten years from the beginning of 1956 to the end of 1965. Rashid said, smiling, 'Great days. Do you remember the Fuhaihil house?'

Khalfan replied, toying with his prayer beads, 'The days of our youth. Who can forget them?'

'Do you remember the man from Ajman who imitated Mahdawi during his trial and made fun of him?'

'Of course I do. We used to kill ourselves laughing. And Salum the Tanker who used to spend all his money going to the pictures. Every day without exception he used to see some film at the cinema.'

'And Abdullah Salim's cooking. The food he prepared was the best I've had in my life.'

'And Khalifa the poet. Every day a love poem. He was in love with his cousin. After he left Kuwait and went back to Dubai he married her.'

'A beautiful tale.'

'But she then left him and ran off with a Beduin.'

'Poor chap. What happend to him after that?'

'He almost went potty. But after a while he heard about what happens in India. Every year he would marry a young girl from Hyderabad or Bombay, live with her for a year or six months and then divorce her. He has already been married more than ten times.'

'And Ahmad Khalid, who used to annoy us every morning, getting us up for the dawn prayers. Whatever happened to him?'

'He became an alcoholic and spends all his time in the bar of a small hotel in Deira.'

'What happened to the praying and all that religious devotion?'

'It all went out of the window. The Devil.'

'And yourself. What about you?'

'I've been all right, thank God. I work in the Ministry of Education and have two tower blocks, one in Deira and one in Dubai.'

'That's great. You saved more than most in Kuwait. And your children?'

'The older one got paralysed in a road accident. I've opened up a small shop to keep him amused. The younger one is your son's friend and is getting married today. I'm very fond of him but he's highly strung and strong willed. He trained to be a pilot and is now in the Air Force. As for the daughters, the older one is a teacher and got married to her cousin. The younger one works in the hospital. She was married for two years and then divorced. She lives with her child at home with us.'

'Why did she get divorced?'

'She didn't get on with her mother-in-law and did everything she could to get out of the house. She couldn't bear it. It seems to me that girls these days are concerned with work and jobs more than with marriage and their husbands. The job has money behind it and the husband is usually penniless, his money going on cars and drink and travelling abroad. And you, how's life treating you?'

'I'm a spendthrift as you know from Kuwait. I love to spend. I like good food and fine clothes. I love the grand and beautiful things in life and all this eats up a lot of money. When I came back from Kuwait I lived for some years in Abu Dhabi almost destitute. Even when I got some compensation money I spend most of it, but six years ago the government committee built for me a huge block of flats and at present I live off the income. In the last few years I've grown accustomed to living more economically but I still love beautiful things. Last summer I travelled to Spain and this year I'm going to Switzerland. They tell me it's nice and peaceful.'

'And your family, how are they?'

Rashid laughed and said, 'A strange business. My father discovered wine ten years ago and is now an addict. We were helpless in offering advice to him. We took him to doctors and men of religion – with his consent – but it was useless. My son is a fundamentalist and forbids the TV in his house. Every year he goes off with Indian and Pakistani members of the Society for the Call to the Religion of Islam. They disappear for two or three months. During that time his wife and children come and live in our house.'

'How extraordinary.'

'My daughter, Nura, has been a teacher for a number of years. She is now the Principal of a secondary school. Unfortunately she has not yet got married. Why should the young men get married when they can go abroad several times a year and take their pleasure of a score of girls? Our country has become strange. Customs have been turned upside down and all the old values have changed. We don't know where we're going.'

The two friends went on talking about their memories and about what had happened to each of them. More people came in and sat down around their table. One of the big merchants came. A number of those present got up and greeted him. After that a senior army officer came in and the same gestures were repeated. There followed a well-known Under Secretary in one of the Ministries. The same greetings were repeated with an increasing number of people. Incense burners were brought in and rose water was sprinkled. The waiters began to put food on the table. One of the guests who was sitting at the table of Khalfan and his friend and devouring plates of harisa placed in front of him, observed, 'The harisa is fine and the roast meat is fine, because they are prepared in the bride's house. But the hotel food is cold and tasteless.'

His neighbours around the table agreed with him and pounced on the roast lamb that was put on the table. After the main meal, sweets were brought in. One man, the most voracious eater of them all, said, 'Our weddings have become feeble and boring affairs, especially those held in hotels. Food only. No music or singing or dancing. Last year I was in Damascus and some Syrian friends invited me to a wedding party. It was one of the nights of my life. Excellent food and music and dancing and gaiety. Everyone there was happy and laughing, swopping jokes and comments.'

He pointed to the other tables.

'Look at the people here. Not one of them is smiling. Long frowning faces as if we were attending a funeral rather than a wedding.'

Rashid laughed at the remark. After a while the guests began to leave the room. The groom and his friends bad the guests farewell at the door. Khalfan and Rashid walked slowly round the room and chided each other for the lapse in their friendship all these years. Each blamed himself for the shortcoming. They promised to renew afresh their old friendship. At the door Rashid kissed the groom and wished him every happiness. He embraced Khalfan and kissed him, tugging at his embroidered bisht. The waiters were cleaning the tables of the large room. Khalfan had the feeling that he would not see Rashid, his friend from Kuwait, ever again.

93

14
Jasmine

I

He was going into the shop as she was coming out. He looked at
her and followed the look with a thousand sighs. He was overcome
by the scent of jasmine. Rashid did not know why he had entered
that particular shop. He seized the first thing that caught his eye,
which happened to be a teddy bear. He paid for it quickly and left
carrying it in his hand. The shopkeeper shouted after him,
wanting to wrap it up for him. He scanned the street in search of
the girl who had beguiled him. She and her mother were getting
into a car waiting for them in the street. The car set off. He ran
after the car in pursuit. After a short while he gave up, out of
breath. What madness had gripped him? He would never be able
to catch up with them. He was in Murshid suq and he had left his
car by the creek to be cleaned by an Indian boy. He thought of
taking a taxi, looked round for one, but as luck would have it, there
were none to be found at that moment. He walked to his car,
depressed but intoxicated by the smell of jasmine. What a paragon
of gorgeous fair humanity he had set eyes on! He recalled the
words of his friend Hamad about how seldom you came across
beauty in our women. If only Hamad had seen this wonderful
work of art, what would he say? And the smile that radiated
happiness and joy, and the eyes – what magic and splendour!
When he reached his car he was full of a sense of tender
wellbeing. He gave the boy who had cleaned his car twenty

dirhams and also the teddy bear. The boy was delighted and muttered his thanks.

Rashid returned to his car to the Gold Suq turning round to the left. Cars were moving slowly. He looked at the sparkling old jewellery on display in the shop windows. His watch showed that it was ten in the morning although the clouds and the drizzle made the suq seem as if it were sunset. Pedestrians thronged the shops. He saw two young women dash into one of the shops out of the rain. He turned right into the street of tailors and saw a girl coming out of one of the shops. She was walking with head erect, firm step, an aba'a over her shoulder and was unconcerned with the light drops of rain that were splashing on her head and face. He did not look at her for long. He was still drunk with the scent of the jasmine girl who had conquered his feelings. He contemplated the stores on his right. There was a silversmith's shop. Who bought silver these days? Indians mostly or Pakistanis. An Indian restaurant displayed sambusa and slices of fried fish. How appetising it was, but whenever he had had some he always suffered from stomach ache. A pregnant woman went by followed by seven small children. Thank God for her. May she carry on her good work. We are in a minority in this country and need a big increase in our numbers. One woman who lived near him had produced fourteen boys and one girl and she was still one of the toughest women in the quarter. How can people say that pregnancy and childbearing takes it out of women and ruins their health?

He turned right into As Soor street. On both sides there were shops and shops of women's clothes. Some traders were taking bundles of clothes inside so they would not get soaked. Others did not bother to bring them in. It seemed that they were cheap dresses and pullovers made of cotton and polyester, rather than silk or expensive cloth. His cousin told him last week that she had bought some organza for a new dress. The price was a thousand dirhams a metre. But she was always boasting like her mother. Since he was small he had hated his aunt and her daughters, stupid, presumptuous loud mouths with tongues of venom that were like the poison of half a dozen vipers and a dozen scorpions. At the end of the road a policeman stopped the traffic to let some pedestrians cross the road. Rashid set off again and turned right to Murshid suq. He went round in a circle a number of times in the hope that he would for a second set eyes on the girl with the jasmine perfume but to no avail. He came back to the suq in the evening and went up and down several times on foot and in the car. He did not see the jasmine girl. He returned the next day and the day after that and for the rest of the week. Not a trace.

On the sixth day when he had almost given up he saw her. The girl and her mother were coming out of one of the perfume shops in Suq Murshid street. He stopped his car in a no parking zone, got out and followed her from the perfume shop to the underwear shop to the toy shop, to the luggage shop, to three shops dealing with women's clothes. They then went into a shop selling refreshments next to the perfume shop. He followed them in and ordered an apple juice. The young lady's mother had her back turned to him but the young lady looked at him and smiled. She was drinking pomegranate juice. Rashid visualised the red juice trickling down her throat and into the whiteness and delicacy of her body. He did not know how he drank his own juice, but it was the most delicious fruit juice he had drunk in his life. The mother settled the bill and the two of them went out. Rashid tossed five dirhams down on the till and walked out briskly after them. A long black Datsun car was waiting for them in the street outside. The mother got in first and then the girl. As she closed the door she gave a broad smile and the car set off. He ran to his own car. When he reached it he saw a huge clamp on the front wheel. He cursed the traffic police, the security and the law. A thousand cars stopped where parking was prohibited and they were concerned only to put a clamp on his lousy car and at this particular time too. When the policeman came to unlock the clamp Rashid was still under the influence of the jasmine perfume. It was definitely love. It was his fate to love that jasmine.

For two weeks he haunted every shop and alley way of Suq Murshid and the Gold Suq morning and evening. There was no trace of the jasmine. At the end of the second week when he was almost in despair he saw their car parked outside a big department store. His spirits rose and he was bowled over at the sight of the black car. He considered going into the store. Not a good idea. The store was large. She might perhaps leave by one of the many doors as he was entering by another door. He would not let the chance slip by this time. He sat in his car, opened the windows and waited for Jasmine to come out with her mother. He did not have long to wait. After ten minutes Jasmine and her mother emerged, loaded with parcels. The driver met them in the middle of the road and took some of the parcels. Rashid longed to carry all the parcels Jasmine was carrying. She was wearing a black dress decorated with red stripes. Her aba'a had fallen to her shoulders. What a beautiful neck! The neck of an untamed filly. And her hair was like a dark waterfall.

The black car moved off and Rashid followed them. They went along Traffic Street and then turned right heading for the Clock Tower Roundabout. They were without doubt going over to Ber Dubai. But no. The car turned to the left heading for the Flame Roundabout. Rashidiya of course. He was right. It was indeed New Rashidiya. Behind their house were sand dunes and the endless stretch of desert. He made a note of the house. On his return to Ber Dubai the car radio was broadcasting one of his favourite songs of Muhammad Abdu. He sang with it loudly and with abandon. He recalled the line of some writer he had read in a magazine, 'Love is like the measles. We all get it in the end.' He realised that he was going down with an attack of the measles of love.

II

He maintained a vigil on the house. He saw a middle aged man drive up in an old American car. He did not stop sounding the horn until the gates were opened. He was of course Jasmine's father. He saw a teenager go in and out frequently with his bicycle. He was of course Jasmine's young brother. His beloved and her mother did not often go out. For a whole week they only went out twice. Once to go shopping and once to a house in the Hamriya quarter, presumably belonging to some relations. On both occasions when Rashid saw Jasmine with her mother in the car from a distance, he caught a whiff of that fragrant perfume which had never left him. Even in that wretched Ministry office which he shared with two of his colleagues he used to savour the smell of jasmine. How Rashid rejoiced in his love. Even the attacks of asthma that he often suffered from became less frequent. He continued to watch the house. It would appear that the family of Jasmine was very conservative. She only left the house with her mother. She did not go to school. Presumably she had completed her secondary education and her family would not let her go on to the university. They were right. The stories he heard about university girls were not at all satisfactory. If his sister wanted to study any subject other than Islamic law and jurisprudence he would not allow her to go to the university.

At the end of the second month of his infatuation with Jasmine he went for a ride with one of his colleagues from work, a sociable cheerful chap who lived in the Rashidiya quarter. They drove round the quarter and talked about all sorts of things. So as not to arouse his colleague's suspicions he pointed to this blue house or that yellow house, or this brown house on the right, or that green house on the left and casually asked who lived there. Were they decent folk or not? His friend answered Yes or No and sometimes elaborated on the merits of the people of this house or on the demerits of the people of that house. On other occasions he just answered Yes or No without any further comment. When the car came near the house of Jasmine's family, Rashid's heart began to beat faster. He pointed to the house. Rashid's colleague replied, 'They're good folk'.

The colleague was content to give only that brief reply. Rashid asked for no further elaboration. The positive remark delighted him. What more did he need? Jasmine's family were good folk.

III

Rashid's mother was a lady with a forceful personality. When she was over thirty she had joined literacy classes and had managed to bring up her children and to continue her education and to complete the secondary stage. He used to love her and fear her at the same time. He summoned up his courage and informed her that he wished to marry a girl from Rashidiya. This did not please her.

'Your aunt has a whole tribe of girls', she replied.

'I don't want to marry one of my cousins.'

'Jumaira is full of girls, our neighbours and our kind of people.'

'I don't want one of the girls of your neighbours or your kind of people.'

His mother tried to calm him down a bit and asked, 'Fine. What's the family of the girl you want to marry?'

'I don't know them.'

She flared up and shouted at him, 'God's truth. You want to

marry a girl from a family you don't even know?'

He repeated what his colleague had said, 'They're good folk'.

'How can you know they're good folk when you don't know them?'

He said with resignation, 'I'm not bothered with the girl's family. It's their daughter I love.'

The mother replied scornfully, 'There's no doubt that this will be one of those telephone infatuation weddings. What's the name of your heart's delight?'

'I don't know.'

When she heard this answer his mother exploded, 'Have you gone mad?' she shouted at the top of her voice. 'You want to marry a girl. You don't know where she comes from, who her family is and you don't even know her name.'

Rashid replied quietly, almost in tears, 'Please, mother, if I don't marry this girl, I shall die'.

Talk of death cooled the mother down. She looked at his woebegone face and recalled his sick childhood and the asthmatic attacks that he still suffered from. Her heart was filled with compassion. She gave him a hug and said tenderly, 'Don't be upset, my child. We'll get you married to her.'

Next day he took his mother and aunt to Jasmine's house. His aunt was grumbling all the time. He put them down at the house and promised to come back and collect them an hour later.

Half an hour later he parked at the house. Twenty minutes before the time was up, his mother and aunt came out and got into the car. When the car set off Rashid showered his mother with a host of questions, 'Do they give their consent? What do they say? Do they want time to take advice? No matter. Have you seen the girl? As sweet as the moon, isn't she? Did they talk about the dowry? I'll borrow the money and pay it back, however much it is.'

His mother firmly interrupted him. 'Gently, gently.'

He carried on talking, 'She's as lovely as the moon, isn't she?'

His mother replied, shaking with distress, 'The girl will not suit you'.

Rashid started and said quickly, 'The girl will not suit me! Don't you want me to be happy? I'll marry her in spite of you.'

His mother said sadly, 'No, no, my dear child. She is ill and although she is twenty years old, her mind is the mind of a child of five.'

15

Look After Yourself

I

'Ass. Ass. Heaven's above, you're a complete ass. You've got the body of an ass. It's four years since you finished your studies and you still haven't got a job yet. All you do is eat and sleep. When are you going to fend for yourself? When are you going to get a job? OK, my circumstances are straightforward enough and I won't need any help from you. But supposing I die tomorrow, who's going to look after your big sister and your aunt? Do you want them to beg?'

Such censorious stern words as these were daily directed by Ahmad al Aryan towards his son, Rashid. It was a one-sided discussion, a monologue. The father talked, blamed, criticised and scoffed. The son sat as silent as stone, unshaken and unmoved by the words of rebuke. The father's words revolved around the same subject with variations, greater or lesser according to how energetic, heated or angry he felt.

'The young men who studied with you, where are they now? Abud al Araj has become an official in the Ministry of Education with a salary of 7000 dirhams, that is twice what I get. Khulud Mashal has been promoted to First Lieutenant in the police force with a salary of at least 6000 dirhams. Khammas ibn Surur Tayzab has ten commercial franchises which he hires out. These bring in more than 20,000 dirhams a month. Ahmadu Hamama has three video shops and two audio cassette shops and has been married twice. And you, Rashid al Aryan, strong bright lad that you are, you have turned into an ass that does no work, only eats and

101

sleeps. What have I done in my life for God to have given me a son that is idle rubbish like you?'

He commented scornfully on his son's hobbies. 'These magazines you read – what use are they? Events, Appointments, My Lady, Hobby, Fishing, Sports Stars, even children's comics, Majid, Samir, Mickey, Superman. Where do you get the money to buy them? Oh, yes, I know, I know. It's that foolish aunt of yours who has spoiled you. Every time she gets an allowance from the Ministry of Social Affairs, she passes money on to you. She's ruined you by doting on you and coddling you. She imagines you will look after her and spend on her in the future. Oh, God help us. You're idle and can't even manage to look after yourself. How on earth could you look after other people?'

Sometimes he criticised how his son passed his time. 'Don't you ever get tired of watching television all those hours? Aren't you afraid of your eyes? You watch everything, religious talks, cartoons, soap operas, Arab films, foreign films, variety programmes, the lot. How can you bear sitting through all those long hours, your eyes glued to that wretched tiresome box?'

At other times he would taunt him bitterly. 'When you get married, your wife will be happy because you'll be a better cook than she is. The only thing that fool of an aunt ever taught you was how to cook. And now you're better than she is in that unmanly activity, Huh! Cooking with foul smelling fish and the odour of onions.'

He tried to interest him in particular jobs and skills. 'Seize your opportunity. You've got the secondary certificate. There are still vacancies for army officers. We've got a cousin who works in the section dealing with recruitment. Go to him. He'll help you. In a year or two you'll be an officer with a star on your shoulder and 7000 a month in your pocket.'

Rashid rejected the idea. He did not like violence or discipline. His father suggested other kinds of work.

'All right, then. You've got an uncle working in the port. It's true that he doesn't like us much and hasn't been to see us since your mother died, but I know he's a good chap. Go to him. When he sees you he'll look after you and help you get a job as a clerk at the least – 3 or 4000 dirhams, less than the army but better than nothing and better than this life of idleness.'

Rashid showed his rejection of this idea by remaining as silent as a stone as he usually did whenever he was unimpressed by what his father said. One day his father made a fresh proposal. He smiled happily.

'Listen, Rashid. My friend Abdullah has told me that the British company he works for his just fired their public affairs officer and that the post is vacant. All you have to do is to take the foreign employees' passports and documents and get their visas, residence permits and work permits from the relevant government department. It's easy work and Abdullah says the pay is good, 6000 dirhams plus extras.'

Rashid did not warm to the idea. He hated the British and detested government departments and all those who worked there.

Another day over lunch his father had another suggestion. 'I was in the bank today. The Pakistani there told me that they need nationals to work with them. When I mentioned you, he was very keen to take you on. The pay's not very good but it gets better. I know one bank manager who started his working life as a messenger in that bank.'

Once again Rashid turned into a stone, but his father did not surrender to despair. Although his son was stupid or backward or unbalanced as far as a job or thinking of his future was concerned, it was his duty to accept him as he was, just as his uncle had accepted his son who was paralysed, or as his aunt accepted her daughter who was dumb. It was a matter decreed on high. These things were sent by God to try us. An affliction from which there was no escape. But then with his son Rashid it was somehow different. For he knew that he was bright. He had always been in the top ten at school and in spite of his aversion to physical violence, nobody was able to get the better of him when he was angry. He had once knocked down a Pakistani porter and fractured his jaw for annoying him. His son was clever and strong but did not want to work in any job or to take up any career. All he wanted was to sleep, to cook, to eat, to watch television and to read magazines.

One evening his father came up to Rashid, took him by the arm and proposed another idea. 'Rashid, you like reading magazines, don't you?'

'Why, yes.'

'Well, today I had coffee at the Fishmarket. I was talking to a chap whose job is dealing with staff at the town hall. He said they need somebody to work in the library. The pay is poor but you like reading magazines. All you have to do is arrange the newspapers, magazines and books and put them back on the shelves in their right places.'

Rashid replied that he did not care for books and turned once again into a silent stone. His father went mad and shouted at him, 'You're an ass. Do you want to spend your life as if you are a mouse in a hole? You've got to look after yourself, you idiot. This life of yours – compare it with what your classmates and friends in this part of town are doing. You're doing nothing at all. Nothing. You don't even live, you're not alive. In actual fact, you're dead. People have forgotten that I have a son.'

Rashid did not say anything. His father went red in the face and went on shouting at him. 'If only you were to get a job. If only you were to get out or get involved in something. Young men smoke. You don't smoke. Young men drink. You don't drink. Young men have affairs. You don't have affairs. Not once have I caught you smoking a cigarette. Not once have you come home at night drunk or under the influence. Not once has the telephone rung, with a woman's voice wanting you. Is this life? You're dead, dead, dead.'

II

When it reaches boiling point, water is changed into vapour. The shouting of Rashid's father on this last occasion reached a point that changed Rashid completely. He started to think seriously about work. He did not like the jobs his father had spoken about or jobs he had thought about. Then one day he went with his aunt to Ber Dubai and passed by one of the popular restaurants there. His aunt said, 'When you get married, we can do some cooking in one of these places. They say that the food is good.'

This remark made him think about a job that he had not considered before. The only thing he was good at was cooking. He began to ask about these restaurants and learned that their owners made huge profits. People ordered food from them for weddings, for celebrations and large parties or for when they went on an outing. He raised the subject with his father who exploded with rage and shouted at him.

'What, you want to work as a cook? What an affliction! This is work for women. Have you taken leave of your senses? Have you forgotten about your family and its standing? Your grandfather was one of the leading pearl fishers of Dubai. And you, his grandson, want to go and work as a chef! What have I done that God has cursed me with a son like you? What would your mother say? That she would rise from her grave and see her son, the apple of her eye, her noble young cavalier, wanting to work in a kitchen! What have we done to you that you will cause ordinary people to laugh at us and chuckle over our misfortune?'

Rashid ignored his father's objections. Indeed the objections strengthened his determination to carry out his plan. He studied the whole matter and how much it would cost. He went to the town hall and obtained a licence to open a popular restaurant. He borrowed 50,000 dirhams from one of the banks. He rented an unpretentious site. He bought a few small pots and stoves. His father became more and more angry but could do nothing at all about it.

III

Within a year Rashid's restaurant became well-known all over Dubai. The quality of the cooking attracted customers from Sharjah and Ajman. The place has expanded and the pots and stoves have increased in size and number. He now has ten people working for him. At first he used to borrow cigarettes from one of his assistants. Now a packet of Marlboro is hardly ever absent from the front pocket of his dishdasha. He has started to drink beer with some friends. On Thursday night when he comes home he is always drunk, singing in a loud voice. His aunt has started to reply to a whole lot of phone calls from female voices, all asking for Rashid. 'No, my dear. No, my dear. Rashid is not in. He's at the restaurant. He'll be back at ten o'clock.'

He now has a good income. His father is still angry but the anger gradually subsides as the income increases.

16

A Late Dinner

Hamad came in making his usual din and clatter. His wife woke up from a settee in front of the television. She looked at the long clock on the wall. Half past two. The television screen was blank. Grey and black lines and dots showed that transmissions for the day were over.

She switched the television off. Hamad came in and shouted, 'Asleep in front of the box as usual?'

'What do you expect me to do?'

'Read *The Three Musketeers* or watch the film *The Children Have Grown Up* on the video or . . .'

'I've read *The Three Musketeers* more than three times and *The Children Have Grown Up* bored me stiff after you watched it almost every week for a whole year.'

'Watch one of the old comedy films of Ismail Yasin.'

'You know I can't stand his films.'

'Listen to the BBC Arabic service.'

'The BBC Arabic service ends at midnight.'

'Listen to the English language service. We've got a huge radio that can pick up all the stations of the world.'

Hamad's wife smiled and said, 'I'm not Mrs Shakespeare'.

'Learn some English.'

'I registered twice at the British Council but you kept forgetting to take me there.'

'Learn English through cassettes.'

107

'You tried to learn French through cassettes without any success.'

'I was lazy.'

'I'm lazier than you.'

'Is it deliberate laziness?'

'In our case, yes.'

Hamad took off his iqal and ghutra and placed them as usual on the coffee table. Drunkenness never affected his spruceness. Almost every night he came home under the influence of drink but never did he come home with his dress disorderly or his hair dishevelled. Sometimes he came home staggering from the effects of liquor but he would take off his clothes in his usual methodical way and place them on the coffee table by the television set. She wished he would eat out for she was in no mood to cook. He looked at her, smiled and said, 'I want some macaroni'.

She had hoped not to have this labour imposed on her. She would have to take the mince meat out of the fridge and soak it in water. The macaroni would have to be washed and boiled. Preparing the gravy with the necessary care and attention would demand enormous effort. Should she refuse on the grounds that it was too late? Should she feign illness and offer a light alternative? Egg and onion or cheese and tomato sandwiches? She had tried this once before and he had been furious with her. The effects lasted for some time. But she surrendered to the macaroni pot. She got up and took Hamad's iqal and ghutra to the bedroom. He put a wrestling tape on the video. André the Giant was being menaced by Hulk Hogan. As his wife went from the bedroom to the kitchen he called out, 'Who do you think is going to win, Hulk Hogan or André the Giant?'

She said crossly, 'Wrestling is a complete farce'.

'What about the chairs they smash over their heads and the blood that pours down their faces?'

'It's a complete and utter farce.'

'But it's great entertainment.'

She was tempted to reply that it was entertainment for idiots and fools but she refrained. She knew that Hamad was extra touchy when he was drunk and would twist anything she said and flare up. As she went into the kitchen she said, 'Each to his taste'.

She took out a packet of mince meat and poured some hot water over it. She took out the macaroni and measured some out into a small pot. What was it she loved in Hamad that led her to marry him? His bushy moustache? His thick sensuous lips? His roving eyes? His generosity? She did not know! Sometimes he got on her nerves so much that she wished she had been a Christian nun who never got married at all. She once complained to her friend Ulya about his inconsiderate way of demanding a hot meal after midight. Ulya guffawed, 'Thank God he only demands a hot dinner and not something else', she said.

She wanted to ask about the something else that other husbands demanded of their wives but did not do so because Ulya could at time be very direct and extremely frank.

Her sister, Fatma, was married to a man who was very domestic. He never stayed up late, never got drunk and never went out at night. He was fast asleep at ten and up at five. He went on trips only with her and never went shopping or on any outing without her. In spite of all this she never heard a word from her sister in praise of her husband or of gratitude to the fates for having sent her such a paragon. Hamad came into the kitchen and sniffed noisily at the cooking smells, 'Did you know that my mum used to call me the kitchen cat?'

She smiled through her anger and annoyance. He took some olives out of a bottle in the fridge.

'I used to eat everything in the kitchen', he said, 'vegetables fruit, stale food, bread and sweets. I used to be crazy about sweets.'

Her irritation returned. She frowned. She took some onions and started to chop them up. Hamad laughed.

'You'll cry', he said.

She glared at him as he laughed.

'Don't get cross. Psychologists tell us that there is something positive about crying. It releases tension and is a safety valve for pressures so people do not explode.'

He took a tomato from the table as he left the kitchen chuckling.

'If I suffered from nervous tension I would take a dozen onions and cut them up with you so I could cry and get relief, but the stories and jokes of the lads this evening were so good that I do not feel any anxiety or tension.'

Under her breath Hamad's wife cursed psychologists, her husband, his friends and the wretched luck that had bound her to a man with such stupid sentiments. As she chopped the onions she cut a finger of her left hand. She opened a drawer, took out a bottle of iodine and dabbed her wound. It stang. She started to cry and the tears of grief mingled with the tears caused by chopping the onions.

Every woman in the city was enjoying pleasant slumber and sweet dreams except her. She was isolated in this unending penance, this exorbitant duty that required her to get up from a delightful sleep, disturbing her night and straining her nerves. She recalled her childhood and the long nights when she slept with her friend, Hind, who lived nearby. Hind had chubby cheeks and a sweet voice. She used to tell her long strange tales about the loves of princes and princesses, about the marvels of jinns and spirits and about fish and snails that could talk and get married and quarrel like human beings. These stories of Hind still amused her. Where did she get them from? After the stories the two friends would snuggle up together and fall into a deep sleep.

Hamad's wife was soothed by these memories and went back to her cooking. The mince meat had thawed out. She put it in the pot and added the onions. The macaroni was boiling in another saucepan. She stirred the mince meat and onions. Hamad may not be an ideal husband but he was generous. Three days earlier he had bought for her a pearl necklace for ten thousand dirhams and on their fourth wedding anniversary he had brought her earrings studded with diamonds and sapphires. The television and video in the sitting room were the biggest size and the latest models on the market in the whole Emirates. When she was a little girl her mother used always to quote the proverb: 'Generous children are the children of God, even if they are sinners.'

Hamad was not a sinner. He went once to Bangkok and came back grumbling and complaining about the heat and squalor and how the yellow races would conquer the world and destroy it. Whenever the husband of her friend, Aisha, came back from one of his many trips abroad he would bring albums full of pictures of the whores of Manila, Bangkok, Bombay or the cities of Europe. He would boast of these pictures especially if there were three or four women present. He was like a cockerel with its comb ablaze. Maybe Hamad had had some fleeting affairs but he never talked about them in front of her or bragged about them. Sometimes he would complain loudy, 'My father married three times and his brother four times. My grandfather had six wives and I've only got one wife, one woman. It's unfair, terribly unfair.'

His wife never took any notice of this moaning which was made jokingly. When he was in an affectionate mood or was feeling cheerful he would say, 'A man is like a dove. The male must have one female only.'

Hamad's wife gradually felt more loving towards her husband as she prepared the macaroni salad which he preferred moderately mixed. Not thick and piled up like some frozen mess dumped on top of the macaroni nor too refined which made it like soup.

She did like her husband's way of eating especially when he was reasonably intoxicated. He would eat with relish, uttering grunts of approval for the cooking and gossiping about the events of the day, recollections of their marriage or of the days when he was a child. He could be very funny when he was taking off his colleagues and bosses at work. Jasim was like a limping duck. Khalifa had a head like a broad watermelon. Salim had a thin voice like a police whistle. Abdullah's face was like that of a kurkumba fish and Khalid's body was as huge as a water tank.

When he was like this she wished their marriage could continue in the same vein to the end of time. What would happen to her if he died or was in one of those awful road accidents which were illustrated in the papers, or had a heart attack like her cousin Ibrahim who was not more than thirty when he died? Or died of hunger or got drowned in a fishing jaunt as happened to the sons of Umm Muhammad who used to live next door to them in the old quarter?!

She shuddered at such gloomy thoughts and tried to banish them from her mind. Her mother used to say that when people thought hard about particular things, they were sure to happen.

Hamad's wife concentrated her efforts on getting the salad ready. Its shape must be regular, architectonic and splendid. She cut the tomatoes into slices and placed them in the middle of the plate with small pieces of lettuce on the right and pieces of cucumber and carrot on the left hand side of the plate. Hamad loved his salad like that.

She then put all the dishes on a tray and hummed one of Rabab's songs.

She took the tray with the late dinner into the sitting room. Hamad was engulfed in deep sleep on the comfortable chaise longue. On the television screen the cat, Tom, was disguised as a beautiful female mouse and was trying to lure the mouse, Jerry, out of a small hole in the wall. Hamad's wife smiled and switched off the television. She took the late dinner back to the kitchen and put a blanket over her sleeping husband.

17
In the Mortuary

The News is Broken

'I'm a murderer, I'm a criminal. I'm the one who gave him a hundred dirhams. If I hadn't given him that money he wouldn't have left the house.'

The girl held her mother tight and said, 'Calm down, calm down, it was the will of God.'

Their neighbour who worked at the hospital and who had brought the news said, 'We must all go off to the mortuary.'

The sister said amid her distress, 'Why should we go to the mortuary? Didn't you identify him?'

'Yes. I did the identification. Tall, swarthy, feeble-minded and always running about the streets of Hamriya. Who else would that describe? But it was an awful accident and his face is smashed up. The police need someone from his family to identify him. That's why I've come to take you to the mortuary. His body is in the fridge there.'

When the mother heard these words she cried out louder and said again, 'I'm a criminal. I'm the cause of his death. Why did I give him a hundred dirhams? Why did I let him leave the house at such an ill-omened time?'

The neighbour said impatiently, 'Let's get to the mortuary and clear the matter up.'

The girl still clung to her mother who went on sobbing and wailing and said, 'But we ought to call by my sister, Fatma.'

113

'And Aisha, my sister,' shouted the mother, 'and our neighbour, Umm Ahmad, must also go with us.'

'And of course,' added the girl, 'our neighbour, Fawzia, as well. She was the only person who had any sympathy for the poor soul. She was always playing with him and calling him: "My darling, my promised one."'

The neighbour got cross and said, 'Why don't you take the whole neighbourhood? What's all the talk about? What are we going to – a wedding party or a mortuary?'

In spite of his protests they passed by the houses of all those women, and the car did not set off for the hospital until they had all been picked up.

On the way to the Mortuary

The mother said through her tears to her aged neighbour, Umm Ahmad, 'Salum asked me for a hundred dirhams to buy a pair of pigeons. I'd promised them to him for a month and done nothing about it until today. If only I hadn't given him the money. He went running off as usual. He never took any notice of anything and as usual raced after the cars. Now they come to tell me that he's in the fridge. A car hit him and killed him.'

Umm Ahmad said, 'Ever since they brought in cars and paved the roads, there's not been a single day without disaster. We were much better off without these lethal things that destroy our children far more than illness or wars did in the old days. And pigeons,' she went on, striking her breast, 'when did the price of a pair of pigeons ever reach a hundred dirhams? It's the end of the world. Incredible, Incredible. A pair of pigeons at a hundred dirhams, it's the end of the world.'

Fawzia wept silently on the back seat. She turned to his sister and asked, 'Did he have any breakfast this morning?'

His younger sister thought for a moment. 'I don't know,' she replied, 'I was asleep when he went out.'

Fatma then pointed at Fawzia. 'Why is this idiot coming with us?' she said angrily. 'Who invited her? Isn't there enough idiocy today?'

'Shame on you,' answered her sister. 'She used to think the world of Salum.'

114

Fatma commented sarcastically, 'God's will be done. You mean, one idiot loves another. Qais and Laila. What a load of nonsense. If only you had brought some man along who would be able to help us at this difficult time.'

The driver cleared his throat. 'Aren't I good enough, Umm Husain?' he asked.

'You're good enough and more. But your virtuous wife isn't good enough for me. She handed the children to you and ran off to live in sin with a helicopter pilot who spirited her away, body and soul.'

The driver bit his lower lip so angrily that it almost bled. But he was unable to make any reply. His ears burnt at her words. It was true that everybody knew the story of his wife, but at such a time and in front of all these women! Umm Husain was a trouble maker. She was getting her own back. She had wanted to marry him. She used to send lots of dishes of tasty food to his house next door. She even used to get up early in the morning and wash his car. But he never married her. He disliked her shrewish tongue and flinched from her aggressiveness towards others. He had preferred another, gentler, politer, a quiet submissive pussy cat. He put his foot down on the accelerator to banish from his mind the turmoil of these distressing memories.

The old woman, Umm Ahmad, did not hear what Fatma said, and went rattling on, 'Salum's grandfather after whom he was named was greedy as far as eating was concerned. If he had had his dinner and there was a chance of a better meal the same evening, he would throw up the first modest meal to make room for the more sumptuous meal.'

Fatma ignored Umm Ahmad and told her mother, 'I was always telling you not to let him go out of the house by himself. You know that he was daft.'

The mother sobbed all the more when she heard these words of censure.

'Yes, I killed him . . . ,' she mumbled. 'I'm the one who sent him to his death . . . I'm the one who gave him a hundred dirhams . . . But you all know that he wouldn't stay in the house . . . All day he would be in the streets and alleys of Hamriya . . . He would run after dogs . . . after cars . . . after motorbikes.'

'And aeroplanes . . . ,' interjected the aunt, Aisha. 'He used even to race after aeroplanes . . .'

The mother went on, 'When he was tiny we would have to hold him down with rope and chains. And what was the result? Nothing at all. All we achieved was injury to his poor little legs.'

'You shouldn't have let him go out of the house by himself,' Fatma said crossly. 'What will people say? You know that there are people about with poisoned tongues. Malicious people will invent stories about anybody. They will say that his mother and sister killed him so they could lay their hands on his inheritance. They'll say that we neglected him so he would die and we could get the land and the shops he inherited from his uncle.'

'Umm Husain, what on earth are you talking about?' her sister asked in disbelief.

'You're just a kid,' Fatma retorted. 'You don't know anything at all about it. I know better than you how vile and blackhearted people can be, what nasty and hurtful tongues they can have. I swear upon my children that they will say we killed him because we were after the land and the shops. Nothing will stop them. Throughout the mourning period and for weeks and months afterwards they will say that his family murdered him.'

This talk reached even the ears of Umm Ahmad. 'Was Salum murdered?' she asked. 'Who killed him? I thought you said that he died as a result of a road accident.'

Fatma lowered her voice and said crossly, 'Don't we have enough problems to deal with? Did you have to bring along this deaf old crone?'

By now the car had reached the hospital roundabout.

In the Mortuary

When the official saw the women he asked, 'Where is his father? Where are his brothers?'

'His father has been in his grave a long time,' Fatma answered. 'His mother did not like giving birth to sons and was satisfied with the one who is now in the fridge.'

The official was shocked at these words and turned to the driver, 'And you. Aren't you a relation?'

The driver shook his head and said, 'No. I'm just a neighbour.'

'Very well, then,' said the official impatiently, 'come with me.'

The mother's weeping got louder. The aunt sobbed. The little sister began to moan. Fawzia was gripping the door, the tears silently pouring down her face. Fatma and Umm Ahmad did not join in the noisy chorus of lament.

Umm Ahmad said, 'Why haven't they brought a man to wash the body. There's a proper way of dealing with everything, even with death. The body should not be left unwashed.'

The three weeping women went to identify the body and Fatma, Umm Ahmad and Fawzia remained in the waiting room. After a while they returned accompanied by the official. The aunt and the daughter were supporting the mother who filled the corridors with her wailing of grief and despair. They sat her down, brought her a glass of water and washed her face with it. The little sister went to the women's toilet to be sick. The aunt was the only one in control of herself. Amid her tears she said, 'Poor fellow. His face was like a lump of dough. He'd even changed colour. He's turned red . . . No . . . He's turned pale . . . His nose is smashed to bits. One of his eyes has come out of its socket . . . Poor little Salum who used to race after aeroplanes and was then knocked down by a car . . . There is no power except that of God . . . God's will be done.'

'Please, aunt,' said Fatma, after she had wiped the tears away from her mother's face, 'There's no need to give us all these details. Not here.'

On the Way Home

The driver was still smouldering over Fatma's taunts. Her tongue spared nobody. They ought to dissolve her tongue in acid used for melting down metal. How did her husband put up with it? He must either be mad or have the patience of Job. He wished it had been her who had died instead of her brother. Poor Salum.

Fatma looked at the driver's iqal and ghutra and the few white hairs that were beginning to show at the back of his head. Of course he must regret not having married her. He would be thinking of the land and the shops. If he had been her husband and she had inherited all that property she would have bought him a Mercedes instead of this clapped out Japanese car. But he had got what he deserved. One of her neighbours had told her that he was born to misfortune. His father had died in the month he was born. He had caused the death of his little sister by spilling a pot of burning oil over her in the kitchen. But why should she worry about him? She should think about her husband and children. Especially her children. It would be her youngest daughter's birthday in three month's time. She would celebrate that happy event in one of the big hotels and invite all her friends and acquaintances with their children. Then there was her big son who was obsessed by cars, magazines about cars, the mechanics of cars and car shows. She would buy him the car that he really wanted. He had been driving his friends' cars for a long time. And she would indulge herself with that necklace she had fallen for as soon as she had seen it in a small jewellers' shop in the Gold Suq. She had been enchanted by its diamonds – small, medium, large, square, elongated, round – and had been captivated by the ruby in the middle of the necklace that was in the shape of a heart and seemed to pulsate with life, charm and allure. She had tried it on a dozen times. She had wanted it passionately but her means were limited and her handbag was empty. The first thing she would do would be to buy that lovely necklace even if she had to have it on credit until the inheritance was settled. All that would now be possible thanks to her dear brother. Poor Salum.

The little sister had recovered her composure as soon as she left the toilet. She was refreshed by the breeze that caressed her face when the car started. She was a student and did not like studying. Two of her friends had already got married. For some time her cousin had dropped a hint about their getting married but he had insisted that she finish her studies. At first he said that her education would help her bring up the children, but she knew that he wanted her to complete her studies so she could work as a teacher and help with the family income. Now with the death of her brother she would be able to get married and would not need the teacher's salary. Poor Salum.

For a long time Aunt Aisha had had her eye on two cows – one was jet black and the other light brown. They belonged to a neighbour of hers. In her view their milk was wholesome, their cheese was a pure delight and their fat had a most refined taste. But they cost a lot – several thousand dirhams. She would stay with her sister all through the period of mourning and receive the visiting mourners. She would do her duty and then drop a hint to her sister about the two cows. Her sister loved her and would not begrudge her those trifling thousands, especially after the death of her beloved son. Poor Salum.

Interminable weeping did not allow the mother to make any plans. And Fawzia's torrent of tears blinded her from seeing either objects or people. Umm Ahmad went on chattering.

'God curse motorcars . . . The days of donkeys and camels were much better . . . We never heard of anybody being run over and killed by a donkey or a camel . . . Today everything leads to death . . . Cars lead to death . . . Aeroplanes lead to death . . . Yesterday on the television . . . An aeroplane crashed and they brought out human bodies as if they were sacks of rice . . . God save us . . . This is the end of the world . . . The whole world has become one huge disaster area.'

Fawzia and Salum

When the procession reached the gate of the residence they could hardly believe their eyes. Under the huge lawz tree was Salum in his milk white thawb with the buttons undone. There was a mixture of feelings – joy, disappointment, delight, disbelief, amazement, shock. Shock was the emotion that was uppermost. There followed a fusilade of comments, one after the other.

'Salum, where were you?'

'Here you are!'

'And the road accident . . . ?'

'Salum, darling, you're all right.'

'What about the body in the fridge?'

'Thank Heavens. My child. My dearest dear.'

'How did it all happen?'

'Where have you been?'

Salum was taken aback by all these questions and demands for explanation, by all these searching female eyes and by his mother who fainted before she reached him. He stammered, 'I . . . went . . . to the pigeon sellers, . . . I told mummy I was going to buy . . . a pair of pigeons . . . look, aren't they beautiful?'

He was holding in his hands two small pigeons, each with a tail like a fan. He smiled and said, 'I'm going to call the male Salum and the female Fawzia.'

18
Fear

The regulars of the Allegiance coffee house liked to concentrate on one particular topic of conversation. Even if the talk wandered from it, it soon came back to that topic. This was because of the personality of Sultan to whom those who came to the coffee house deferred. All revolved around him, for he was the life and soul of the place. He had an imposing personality which dominated all the others in a number of ways. If people were talking about something in particular he would not switch to something else and would want to make the biggest contribution to any conversation. It was not at all strange if one evening the talk would all be about television programmes, or about the latest models of cars, or about football matches. Some newcomers to the coffee house found this restricting at first but after a few days they knew that they had either to get used to the way that conversation revolved around one subject, the way Sultan preferred, or to leave the coffee house and not come back. And this is what many people did.

One remarkably humid autumn evening Sultan drank a little of the tea that was in front of him and embarked on a discussion, saying, 'We've become like the people of Chicago and New York. Have you seen today's papers?'

Some answered 'Yes' and some answered 'No'. Sultan carried on talking, 'They killed a man after torturing him horribly. They stubbed their cigarettes out in his eyes.'

121

Hamid had not read or heard anything about this crime. He was surprised and wondered, 'When and how did this happen?'

Sultan said, 'A couple of days ago. After they killed him they mutilated his corpse. They cut his head off. We've turned into wild animals. There's been an increase in frightful crimes.'

Abdullah, who liked to offer some opposition to the remarks and views of Sultan, said, 'There's nothing new in this. Violence will always be part of the deep-rooted behaviour of mankind. My grandfather told me about the crimes of the Bedu bandits they used to guard against when he was a lad. They used to kill people horribly, robbed and plundered, and committed awful deeds.'

'In those days there were reasonable pretexts for crime. They killed and stole because they were hungry. Their crimes had some purpose. This man who has been murdered was poor.'

'Maybe,' said Abdullah, 'he was one of those wealthy beggars who bury hundreds of thousands of dirhams under a tree in their back garden or sew them into a mattress.'

'That has not been established.'

'Perhaps there was something else. Wine, drugs, gambling.'

'All these things need money, energy and youth,' said Sultan. 'The man who was killed was old, poor, lonely and crazed. You haven't understood this phenomenon. We now live in big cities crowded with people, competing and fighting with each other and going round the bend. Like in the big cities of Europe and America. You're now finding crimes among us that are motiveless, crimes without any rhyme or reason in them, crimes committed for the sake of fun.'

Sultan's words struck fear into the heart of Hamid. He thought of his wife alone in their flat. It was ten months since they had got married. His father had wanted them to live with the family in his large house which he had designed so it would be big enough for his three sons. Each son was to have a wing of the big house with three bedrooms and a main room each. Right from the beginning his wife had not been happy with this arrangement. She had been very much ill at ease. She told him that she respected his father and mother, his brothers and sisters, but really she could not live with them in one house. She felt stifled by the big house. It was oppressive. She would always have to be fully dressed. She could not walk around the house or in the garden wearing a light dress. The presence of the family inhibited her from laughing and joking, from gossiping and acting spontaneously. She had to weigh every word or remark and consider when she laughed because she was afraid it could be interpreted in a way that could harm her.

At first Hamid was upset by his wife's point of view but he sympathised after a while. She was right. She had not left one family house full of her brothers and sisters just to move to another house full of sons and daughters. Every young wife wanted her own house to furnish according to her own taste and to beautify in the way she chose. She should feel at home in it with her husband without fear of being observed. When he told his father of his wish to move away, he had to face a storm of anger. But his mother managed to persuade him. His father agreed to build a small villa for Hamid and his wife in one of the new districts. The designer and contractor needed a whole year to complete the project. Even after the work had begun, Hamid felt he had to move out of the family house. He moved to a flat in a block belonging to one of his father's acquaintances.

There he noticed the change that came over his wife. Once she had moved into the small flat, she became much more relaxed and free from the gloom, the tenseness, the anxiety and the moodiness that had dogged her throughout the three months they had spent in his father's house. In the new flat she felt liberated in her natural and joyful way. She started to laugh and gossip and joke. She began to eat food she used only to nibble at in the old house. Her cheeks bloomed and liveliness lit up her countenance. She began to work energetically and with enthusiasm and refused to allow him to bring in a servant to help her. If he had known earlier that she would be so transformed he would not have remained in his father's house a single day after they had got married. But these crimes they were talking about.

Sultan said, 'Crime is on the up and up. Murder. Theft. Robbery. Forgery.'

'Have you heard of the naked black robber who greases his body all over before raiding the houses he wants to rob?' asked Abdullah.

Hamid was very much alarmed. 'Why does he do that?'

'So he can't be caught.'

'They grabbed hold of him four times but each time he slipped away thanks to the grease,' added Sultan.

Hamid had visions of a naked black giant coated with grease

that dripped off his body. He had a thick beard, a bald head and terrifying eyes. Abdullah said, 'In the old days thieves used to rob houses that were empty. But now they raid houses that are lived in and areas that are full of people.'

'There was one who used to drug the people in the houses he was going to rob,' said Sultan.

'What about the four youths who raped the Indian girl?' asked Khalfan.

'Crimes just like in the American movies,' commented Hamid.

'Yes. I told you,' went on Sultan. 'Our cities have become crowded and polluted and crazy. These are natural things and will increase in the future. Even the horrifying crimes we see on the TV or read about in the papers, like the Englishman who opened fire on shoppers at the supermarket and filled their bodies with lead, or like the American who shot his wife and children and also the children of his neighbours. All this insane light-hearted killing will be with us before long.'

Abdullah said, 'Don't exaggerate, Sultan. I don't think things will reach such a barbarous state of affairs with us.'

'Steady on, steady on,' said Sultan emphatically, 'In a few years we will become like them and then you mark my words. I'm not exaggerating. This is the natural course of events. When people used to live in villages and small towns they used not to know this kind of crime. It was the theft of a chicken, simple disputes, passing feuds. But when the cities have become large and crowded and full of pollution, disputes and feuds between people have intensified and there has been an increase in crime and now we've got the whole lot. I remember when I was a boy, there was one case of murder and all Dubai shook from one end to the other. People went on talking about it for years. Even simple thefts used to preoccupy people for months. But as for nowadays, there are in one year dozens of murders and robberies, rapes and drug offences. We read about them in the papers and forget about them the same day. People don't care any more. These crimes have become everyday events that rouse no interest at all.'

At these last remarks Hamid became more than ever concerned for his wife. He quickly drank his tea and got up to go to his car. Abdullah asked him, 'It's still only half past ten. It's early.'

Hamid said, excusing himself, 'I'm sorry. I'm tired. I've got a lot on my mind and I ought to get to bed early.'

II

On the way back to the flat Hamid was filled with the gloomiest of thoughts. The naked black robber who greased his body. The criminal who drugged his victims. The youths who raped the Indian girl. He recalled the film, 'Death Wish', in which evil men attacked the family of the actor, Charles Bronson, and raped his family and shattered them psychologically. He drove faster. Why did he agree to their leaving his parental house? There he could have left her in the protection of his family. He could not forgive himself if some awful accident occurred. His dear sweetheart. All that loveliness and delicacy. She could not bear the slightest violence. When he held her tender little hand he felt that if he pressed it too hard the tiny bones would be crushed in his hand. When he hugged her he was afraid of straining her little neck. She only weighed fifty kilograms. She must put on some weight. If she caught a heavy fever she would not be strong enough to withstand it. He overshot the traffic lights. There were no cars coming. What would happen if a police patrol saw him? He would say he was in a hurry. There was an emergency. Let them impose a fine for committing an offence. What did it matter?

When he reached the flat the lights were dimmed. His wife was washing her face in the bathroom. He sat getting his breath back in the living room. When she left the bathroom he put his arms round her and kissed her freshly washed cheeks and smelt her warm soft neck which gave off a soothing scent of pure sandalwood. She asked him with apparent surprise, 'You're back very early this evening.'

'My love. I was dying to see you. From now on I will not go out in the evenings until we have moved into the new villa and until we have taken on a female servant who can stay with you, help you and keep you company.'

III

'Hallo, Khalifa?'

'Yes, my love. This is your darling Khalifa.'

'Listen, do you know what happened yesterday?'

'No, what happened?'

'Hamid returned just seven or eight minutes after you brought me back.'

'Did he notice anything?'

'No, he didn't. I was taking off my make-up and having a wash in the bathroom.'

'Well, that's all right then.'

'True, but in future we're going to have to meet in the morning or afternoon. We're not going to be able to meet in the evening any more.'

19
Influence

Huda was enchanted by the voice of the broadcaster presenting the women's programmes. She was fascinated and obsessed by its sweet melodic rhythms. There was no discordance. It rose and fell with regularity. A smooth voice, a voice of velvet and silk. A warm voice, a voice of Arab coffee and cardamon. What she said was logical, serious, comprehensive, and simply made sense. It was the voice of a woman who knew what life was all about in every detail. Huda tried to understand how she managed to come out with all these admirable things. Had she had a lot of experience in love? Had she been married several times? Had she tasted the bitterness of failure and the sweetness of success? Had she been influenced by the personality of her mother? She certainly had to have been a lady of sensitivity and common sense. Had she benefitted from the personality of her father? He must have been a thoughtful and cultured gentleman. She did not know! Huda's mother was a gracious lady whom she loved dearly but she was really quite ordinary. She did not come out with proverbs and wise saws. When she was angry and berated one of her younger brothers, she would shout, 'Dog, swine. You've just been picked up off the streets. Filthy dirty child. God damn the day I gave birth to you. I wish you had been aborted and you'd never been born.' .,

And her father too was a gentle soul but if he got cross with one of his young sons he would rage at them, 'You vile nasty creatures. You're just riff raff. May God curse your crazy mother.'

There was no doubt that this gorgeous broadcaster had been

brought up in a household that never used such crude and vulgar expressions. All their talk must have been refined and courteous in which consideration was shown for the sensitivities of their sons and daughters who would be spared hearing anything that was hurtful. Their voices even in anger must have been raised only by a fraction of a decibel.

Huda believed that the nicest things the broadcaster said dealt with marriage and the ideal marital life. The many precepts offered in this respect contained the soundest good sense. Huda's ears would be glued to the radio. Her mind would absorb everything she heard and she would try hard to carry out the good advice.

On one occasion the broadcaster said in her daily series dealing with successful marriage, 'Do not spend a lot of time talking to the love of your life on the telephone while he is at work in his office. Such conversations interfere. They embarrass him and can have an adverse effect on his productivity and might delay his promotion and his progress up the professional ladder.'

For three days Huda refrained from phoning Khalfan in his office at the Ministry. On the fourth day he got in touch with her and said angrily, 'Who's been leading you astray?'

'Who's been leading me astray?'

'Yes, leading you astray. For three days you have not got in touch with me here at the office.'

'But, my love, we talk for hours outside working hours.'

'That's not enough.'

'I'm afraid our long conversations may affect your productivity and work.'

He burst out laughing and said, 'My productivity and my work! Who told you we produce anything or do any work in our department. We're just employed here to get our salaries at the end of the month. No more. No less. If you manage to get one or two things done in a day that is a gigantic task that merits reward.'

'If you spend a lot of time talking on the telephone, your promotion may be delayed.'

He burst out laughing again and said, 'Who told you that promotion in our sphere of work or in our establishment had anything to do with work or conscientiousness or effort? The basis for promotion is sucking up to the boss, playing cards with him at his majlis, seeing him off at the airport and being there to welcome him back again, praising his manliness, flattering his taste, lauding his intelligence, looking after his interests, getting his affairs sorted out. These are the things that make for rapid promotion. All the rest is of no importance or value.'

At the beginning of the year the broadcaster's voice whispered with her velvety silky tones into Huda's ear, 'Help your husband to decide the course he wants to take, and to clarify what he wants out of life. Let him identify a goal and progress towards it. When your goal has been reached then set up another one. Work out a plan for the future in stages, each stage to be for five years.' That night after they had talked about how the suffocating humidity was going on and on, she asked him what his goal in life was. He was puzzled, 'What do you mean?'

'What do you want to do in the future? What are your hopes, ambitions, dreams?'

He laughed and said, 'My hopes are as follows: to buy one big Mercedes and one Ferrari sports car. To build up a superb palace with a huge garden overlooking the sea. To own a great big yacht. To visit every country in the world.'

Huda said in a serious tone, 'And how are you going to achieve these goals?'

Khalfan said, smiling, 'Simple. I'll rob a bank.'

Huda felt depressed by his scornful way of dealing with such an important subject. She spoke to him about defining objectives and the necessity of a plan for the future in stages, each stage to be five years. Khalfan laughed and said, 'What strange talk. Defining objectives? A plan for the future? Each stage to be five years? Where do you get such absurd notions from? And who am I to have objectives and plans that stretch for years? I don't know what I'm going to do this evening. Forget all this fantastic nonsense.'

Huda's ears went back to soaking up the broadcaster's words which turned on how the wife should encourage her husband to broaden his culture, exercise his mind and improve his skills. Huda said to Khalfan, 'My love, why don't you finish off your university studies?'

'God help us. I could hardly believe it when I had done with wretched books and boring lectures, with sterile enquiries, abstruse lectures and uncouth students. And now you want me to go back to all that nonsense. God help us. God help us. Don't you have anything better to say than that? It's so boring.'

129

'All right. All right. Don't get cross. Why don't you go to one of the institutes and study accounts or computing?'

'I've been as thick as two short planks all my life as far as figures and maths is concerned.'

'The English language is the language of today. It's the language of commerce, the language of travel, the world language. Why don't you study English at the British Council?'

'A splendid idea. I'll then be able to chat up all the pretty English girls.'

Khalfan's enthusiasm did not last long and Huda did not press him further to master the language of Shakespeare and Chaucer.

The broadcaster talked about the ideal wife and how she should be able to attract the attention of her husband all the time. She gave lots of good advice such as, 'Share in his hobbies.'

Khalfan had two hobbies that he loved. Fishing and going to football matches. The first was a man's world and there was no place for women. Huda did not like fish. Scraping fish, removing the skin and cutting them up were tasks her mother made her do when she was a girl. For her they were utterly repulsive tasks. But the second hobby was open to anybody to pursue and to take an interest in. She began to force herself to watch local matches on television. She did not like the commentaries. There was much faked sentiment and excitement. But she put up with it and suppressed her own feelings. She took to reading the sports pages in the newspapers and magazines. She discovered a strange world of men of varying degrees of fame. There were quarrels and controversies. It was a world with its rites and its customs and its special laws. She already knew the club Khalfan supported. She praised the famous players of the team.

He replied testily, 'These players you mention are not fit to play in the alleys.'

Huda was taken aback and said, 'But don't you support their team?'

'Oh yes. I support their team but they are hopeless players.'

'Why are they famous then?'

'Fame in sport has nothing to do with skill in playing. Being on excellent terms with the managers and the sports journalists and other things have more to do with it.'

She spoke of some European players. He laughed and said, 'You're pronouncing all their names wrong.'

'That's the way they pronounce their names on TV.'

'Whoever said that TV broadcasters are experts in foreign languages?'

She enthused about one local match and told him of her enjoyment of the game. He shouted at her, 'What? That a good match? Are you crazy? It was the worst match I've ever seen in my whole life. The players ran about as if they had two left feet. They kicked the ball into the air all the time as if they were aiming at a goal in the moon. There was no skill. There was absolutely no technique. A boring lousy match. But what do you know about the art of football?'

These blunt remarks crushed any interest Huda had in Khalfan's hobbies.

After breakfast Huda turned the radio on. First, the broadcaster talked about the progress of children at school. Then she went back to offering advice about marriage. She said, 'Don't be jealous and don't spy on all his movements.'

Huda gave up talking to Khalfan about her friend who had seen him in the Gold Suq or her sister who had spotted him in the Trade Centre or about the people who had seen him chasing girls at the Expo Centre. And similarly she showed no interest when he spoke of the pretty Lebanese girl he saw at the pizza restaurant or the charming Indian girl who sat by him at the office in the Department of Immigration or the sweet Philippino girl who served him food at the Sheraton Hotel. He was annoyed at this new way of treating him with indifference and grumbled, 'You've gone off me.'

She was dismayed and said, 'What do you mean?'

'You're not jealous of me any more. It no longer concerns you that I like some other woman. Your ardent passion for me has cooled. You've moved away from me.'

'Don't hurt me with fantasies and delusions, please.'

'They're not fantasies.'

'They are and there's absolutely no ground for them. I love you more than any man in the whole world. You are my life. You are everything to me.'

'That's not true. Not true at all. The woman who is not jealous does not love.'

Huda rapidly went back to making remarks and comments about where Khalfan went and whom he saw.

She sought more advice. The broadcaster was not tight-fisted in offering it.

'Cultivate in yourself a spirit of playfulness. Men love witty women who bring gaiety into their hearts with talk full of merry quips.'

Now Huda was not dull, but neither was she frivolous. She wished she was like her friend Alya who no sooner sat down somewhere than she made everybody curl up with laughter all the time. She started to read books of jokes. She told Khalfan some of the stories of Joha. He said sarcastically, 'I heard those stories when I was still at my mother's breast.'

She told him the jokes she read in *A Thousand and One Jokes*. He commented, 'The jokes of the elephant and the ant are so often repeated that children don't even laugh at them.'

She started telling him a new story she had heard from one of her brothers. He stopped her in the middle and went on to tell the rest of the story. She gave up trying to be funny or to tell jokes.

These discouraging consequences did not destroy Huda's devotion to the dulcet tones of the beloved broadcaster with her broad experience and her many wise words of good counsel. But she hesitated about putting the advice into practice until one day she heard advice that struck a special chord in her heart and plucked at a sensitive string in her bosom.

'Complete frankness, unequivocal standpoints and firm decisions are the foundations for successful marital relations. Be frank with him about what you harbour in your heart. Ask him to adopt clear standpoints about events in your life. Tell him to take firm and bold decisions in the interests of the love of you both.'

She picked up the telephone and dialled him at work. He was surprised that she was contacting him. After the customary greetings she said in a voice full of all the gravity and affection that she was able to muster, 'Khalfan, my love. You know how much I love you. I have never loved anyone before you and I'll never love anyone after you. My life is yours. My whole existence is yours. But you must be absolutely frank with me. You must make your position absolutely clear and take a firm decision. When are you going to see my family and arrange our engagement? When are we going to be married? State the place, choose the time. I love you and will wait for you. But you have got to decide. After one month. After six. After one year. But you have got to be straightforward with me, take up a clear position and be decisive.'

20
Problem and Solution

I

Shamsa is a successful teacher working in a secondary school. She is successful because in teaching history she uses her fertile imagination to transform dry historical facts and events into interesting and diverting stories that arouse the curiosity of her pupils. This gift for telling a story is derived from her family. When her father heard some anecdote, even if it was quite ordinary, he would add to it and embellish it and tell it again to the family in a dramatic way that was absolutely enchanting. Her brother and her mother also had this gift to some extent but not to the extent of her father or herself.

She had been in her profession for four years. At first she used to grumble about little things such as the behaviour of the girls or the teachers or the school servants. Many of the girls were highly strung and were not interested in what they wore or in the tasks they had to perform. They would not study things seriously. Some were quarrelsome and seemed determined to be irritable. In the course of time she realised that such behaviour had hidden explanations which when apparent no longer caused any surprise. Samira, for example, was highly strung because she was having a liaison with a young man and was sending him love letters which he used in order to apply emotional blackmail on her to continue the relationship. And Suad was not interested in clothes, for her family shared a two-roomed house with seven others and there was simply no room for a large mirror. And Najwa was quarrel-

133

some because she disliked her swarthy complexion and crinkly hair.

What disgusted Shamsa most at first was the gluttony of her fellow teachers. Many were always eating sandwiches. Some would bring in cooked food, macaroni and rice and meat and cakes and so on. Sometimes she would see her colleagues lie down in the staff room and have a nap after the fourth lesson of the day. But then what was to be expected from people who ate all that fattening food? She was terrified of the school servants. On one occasion a short servant stopped at the door of the staffroom where Shamsa was sitting with some colleagues and bawled out, 'When you leave make sure you close all the windows and clean the tables and when you shut the door leave the key on the lower shelf outside, not on the upper shelf.'

The head servant, Khamisa, was the dragon of the school. Everybody was scared of her, even the headmistress. She used to bring her own Indian servant along with her to school to carry out the tasks of cleaning and carrying papers and files around the place. Khamisa was a businesswoman. She used to cook for weddings and trade in visas and owned a fleet of taxis. She worked at the school for the sake of appearances only. All these things Shamsa in time took for granted and they no longer upset her. Events and celebrations passed by in a routine manner. The girls studied, left school and got married or went on to the University. It was rare that anything out of the ordinary took place. Once she came across a love letter written by one of her pupils. She was dismayed and the girl began to cry. What should she do with the letter? Should she take it to the headmistress? Should she send for her family? She thought about it for a while and in the end tore the letter up. She kept her lips sealed about the whole matter, as did the girl who wrote it. On another occasion the school was much disturbed when a pupil was involved in a road accident. She had been out with a young man in the middle of the day when she should have been at school. The girl's family threw the blame on the school. The school threw the blame on the girl's family. In time the matter was forgotten because it ended in wedding bells once the two lovers had recovered from the accident. Apart from that, events passed calmly and leisurely for most of the days, and excitedly and frenetically on the days of terminal or annual examinations.

II

One evening Shamsa was browsing through a weekly magazine. She read the section about personal problems. She was amazed at the variety and number of them. It is true that Shamsa was thirty two years old and was still unmarried. But she was content in her professional life and with her family and friends. She was also surprised at the replies. She thought, why should she not write up a particular problem, send it to the magazine and see what the reply would be. She started writing the first letter in the staffroom. After a while one of the teachers came in. Shamsa slipped the letter into her handbag and took it home where she finished it.

The First Letter

'I am writing this letter to you, because my husband and I are suffering acute pain and embarrassment. Our problem is difficult and abstruse. We do not think there is any solution. I was born twenty five years ago, an orphan or a semi-orphan. I never knew my father and I learned later that he left us and went to live in another Gulf state. My mother brought me up excellently and gave me an education. I completed the secondary school and then got a job in a hospital so I was able to pay something back to my mother, for we were in straitened circumstances. At the hospital I got to know a Gulf man who worked in a department next to mine. He was a good man, gentle and pious. He asked my mother if we could become engaged. She agreed and gave us her blessing. We got married even though he was a year younger than me. We had five years of unbroken bliss that nothing was able to upset. He made up for the lack of a father and provided the blessings of a family. We had three sons and a daughter. One terrible day my husband's maternal aunt came to see us from their country – his father had died when he was small and his mother was killed in a road accident. From her we learnt that his father was my father. When he went to that other country he changed his tribal name. My husband is my brother. Since we have become aware of this we have been suffering the utmost anguish. We do not know what to do or how to cope.

Pained and Perplexed.'

This was a complex and difficult problem which the journalist who wrote the replies would not be able to solve. She looked out for the magazine to which she had sent the problem and a fortnight later came the answer.

Reply to the First Letter

'To Pained and Perplexed.

Strange coincidences happen in this world. Your problem is perhaps one of those strange coincidences. There are two aspects of the problem from which you are suffering. First, the religious and legal aspect. Jurisprudents would consider this marriage of yours as one of judicial error. It can legally be dissolved when one of the partners knows that he is not permitted to have married the other. The children are legitimate. You can bequeath things to them and they can inherit from you. Secondly, the psychological and social aspect. It is best for you both to get married afresh and for each of you to find a new life and a new family and may God prosper you.'

It was so easy. Shamsa had imagined that it was a complicated and insoluble problem. She must devise another problem for another magazine.

The Second Letter

'I am a lady, twenty-one years old. Four years ago I married one of my relations. He is a handsome, athletic and well brought up young man with a good income. He has put me into a fine house and has bought me clothes that fill several wardrobes. He has

136

taken me to many of the capitals of Europe and of Asia. He has given assistance to my father professionally and to my brother in completing his university studies. I love him dearly and have a great affection for him. But the problem is that from the first day of our marriage until now as I write this letter he has not performed his rightful conjugal duties. I am still a virgin. I go to the wedding parties of my friends and relations and am filled with envy of them. I am embarrassed, distressed and mentally confused. Please guide me to a solution.

Virgin in Distress.'

A different kind of problem. Two weeks later Shamsa read the following reply in the magazine.

Answer to the Second Letter

'It is clear that you are a nice girl, because it appears from your letter that you have not spoken to your husband about the matter. The solution is in your hands. It is possible for you to advise him to seek the advice of a specialist in nervous and sexual ailments. If it turns out that his affliction is permanent then the ball is back in your court. You are able to seek a divorce on the grounds of his impotence, or you can carry on living with him if your love for him is stronger than anything else.'

A cold reply. She must try another problem and another magazine.

The Third Letter

'I have thought a great deal before writing to you about the problem I am suffering from. I thought I would overcome the problem by myself. But to my great regret I have been unable to and I think I have reached the stage where I need help. Two years ago I got married to my cousin. He is a nice young man with a respectable social position and all sorts of estimable qualities. But

I discovered a year ago that he has been deceiving me. I heard him talking on the phone to another woman very affectionately. I decided to get my revenge and have deceived him once, twice, three times until my reputation has spread. I have many admirers and have had lots of telephone chats and also rendez-vous. Each time I tell myself that it will be the last time, but I go back and do it again. Believe me, I feel great embarrassment about these relationships when I decide to abandon them and return and be faithful to my husband. But each time I am weak and yield to temptation. What do I do? Please guide me to the right answer.

Worried.'

Answer to the Third Letter

'You made up your mind about your husband's fidelity from a telephone conversation without checking up on the matter. You have simply betrayed him and your wrongful behaviour has continued for a whole year. What can I say to you? You have committed offences against yourself, against your husband and against your family and children. You are now suffering but when your husband hears about it your suffering will increase because you have sinned against him and against your family. Abandon this mistaken way of life that you are leading and return to the path of righteousness and bear in mind that God is forgiving and merciful.'

Shamsa continued to send her problems and her stories to different magazines, both regional and pan-Arab. Each time there was a fresh problem and a new story. She derived much amusement from reading the replies.

On one occasion she sent the following letter to the editor of the 'Dr. Lonely Heart' page:

'I am a lady aged twenty-eight, attractive and well-educated. I have got a secondary school certificate. My husband died a year ago and left me a lot of money, which was added to the sum already left to me by my father. But what is the use of the millions, the money, the real estate, so long as I have an empty heart? When I walk in the suqs people's looks follow me around. Some young men who want a passing fling get in touch with me but they do not want marriage, its sanctity or its responsibilities. I feel helpless and fear for myself lest I go astray or yield to temptation. Please advise me as to what I should do.

Lonesome.'

When she looked through the Dr Lonely Heart page three weeks later she did not see her letter published. She found instead the following remark at the bottom of the page next to the short answers to problems:

'To Lonesome.

In view of the delicacy of your problem, please send your address so that we can send you a personal letter which will include the solution.'

Shamsa was taken aback and curiosity prompted her to send her address to the magazine. A week later she received the following letter:

'To my dear Lonesome,

I have read your letter ten times and I am in pain for what you have gone through. I am a young Arab man, forty-five years of age. I divorced my wife after many problems. She was the cause of them all and our only daughter lives with her. I now live in an emotional wilderness. My life and spirits need a sympathetic and kindly lady to share the burden of life in which we can divide up our troubles, our problems and our joys. We can live a life of love and mutual support over which we can fly the flag of felicity and affection. I offer you marriage, love and loyalty to the end of time.'

In the envelope she found the name and address of the journalist, 'Dr Lonely Heart', and with it his photograph. He was fat, wore square glasses and was half bald.

21
The Light that Shines No More

We had checked in and were sitting in the departure lounge. My older brother, Khalid, went off to buy some cigarettes, chewing gum and magazines from the duty-free shops. I looked at the faces of the other passengers. Anxiety, fear, tension always seemed to be apparent in their faces. They try to conceal it by exaggerated activity or by exaggerated idleness, by inspecting their baggage, by nattering, by shouting at children or by flicking through newspapers. Anxiety about unforeseeable aspects of the trip. How many disasters do we see on the television screens each year?! Fear of the unknown. What will happen to them in the foreign land they are going to?! Tension at leaving behind familiar faces, places and daily routines. I looked at the face of my father sitting in front of me in his wheel-chair. If I had sat him down on one of the airport seats, anybody quickly passing by would not have considered that there was anything unusual about him. Since early morning my mother had been getting him ready for the trip. She had bathed him and cleaned him. She had trimmed his beard twice with enormous care. She had polished his moustache. She had wanted to henna his beard and moustache but he had refused, saying in his weak and broken voice, 'No, no henna . . . when . . . I was . . . a young man . . . but not now . . . now that I'm an old man.'

Before his stroke six months ago he used to dye his hair and to apply to that task an art and a skill that exceeded those of a professional barber. After his stroke he refused absolutely to have

141

his hair hennaed. Mother said to him, 'But you're going to London.'

He was adamant. My older brother, Khalid, said facetiously, 'Don't forget. There are those gorgeous English girls.'

Father made no comment. He looked at him unsmilingly and said nothing. I have always felt that Khalid never stops talking. He wants to say something witty and pleasant but it always come out as unfunny and tactless.

Mother dressed him in a white thawb and a grey woollen jacket. My brother said, 'But it's warm.'

She whispered to him sharply and angrily, 'But you're going to London where it's cold according to your sister who has been living there with her husband. And Father is a sick man.'

Mother placed on his head the skullcap, red ghutra and the iqal and brought him a mirror so he could look at himself. She added some sandalwood perfume and some of his favourite French scent for men. Then she dowsed him with some incense. My brother then came out with one of his untimely remarks,

'Father has become a young bridegroom, thank the Lord.'

There was silence. Nobody made any comment. My brother felt embarrassed and left the room.

The announcer's voice added to the din in the departure lounge. It asked us, passengers bound for London, to make our way to one of the doors. Khalid had not come back. I felt irritated at his delay. When he came I told him off but he said, 'There's still half an hour to take off.'

'That's all very well, but father needs special arrangements.'

'Fear not. I've fixed everything with the airline.'

We got going and made our way to the departure gate. We placed our hand luggage on the conveyor belt. I pushed Father's wheel-chair. The security officer stopped us and began to search Father, going through his pockets. My brother said to the security officer, 'Fear not. He's not well, he's paralysed. He's incapable of hijacking the plane.'

I was annoyed at what my brother said. There was no need for such a remark. The security man said, 'God will see that he gets well, but these are security measures, essential for the safety of all.'

We carried Father still sitting in his wheel-chair down the concrete steps. In the big room on the ground floor we sat waiting for all the other passengers and for the bus that was to take us to the aircraft. Khalid smoked nonstop. He was manifestly unhappy about the whole trip. He had wanted to take his wife and family to Spain. Almost everything had been arranged. He was wanting to go to Barcelona because a friend of his had praised it saying that of all the cities of Spain it was the cleanest, the most advanced and the most beautiful. His wife had wanted to go to Andalusia – to Granada, the Alhambra, Seville. They had decided to spend one week in Barcelona, one week in Madrid and a fortnight in Andalusia. When I told him I wanted to take Father to London for a check-up and treatment he tried to dissuade me at first. He said, 'Haven't we taken him to every hospital in the Emirates?'

'Yes.'

'Haven't we let every famous doctor here see him?'

'Yes.'

'Didn't we ask them if he should have treatment abroad and they all answered that he could not have any treatment better than he was getting from them?'

'Yes.'

'What's the point of going then?'

'I've read in a scientific journal that there are some new drugs for dealing with strokes. Even if we don't get any good from the treatment he will get some comfort from the trip and from sightseeing.'

'But he'll get tired and that may not be good for him.'

'I will look after him carefully.'

When he was quite sure I was determined to take Father to London he insisted on postponing his family holiday and going with us. Why? Did he want to prove that he loved Father no less, cared for Father no less, was dutiful to Father no less than myself? I do not know. He had always been closer to Father. He was the first son and had been indulged. Father gave him the best toys and took him to majlises and wedding parties. The bus arrived. The man standing at the exit called out, 'Transit. Transit. Let the transit passengers come forward first.'

Passengers holding plastic tickets moved forward and went out. Our turn came. We pushed Father's wheel-chair and left with the other passengers. We got on to the bus. When we reached the bottom of the aircraft we waited until all the passengers had gone up the steps. It was very hot and the humidity was stifling. A steward came up to us and said apologetically, 'The lift for taking up disabled or paralysed passengers is being used. We can help you get your father in his chair up the stairs into the plane.'

Khalid said angrily, 'Didn't we tell your office about my father's condition? Each time you said that the arrangements would be carried out completely and comprehensively.'

The steward repeated his apology. With great difficulty we managed to take the chair up. Father was upset and tried to grab the handrail of the stairway. We had to get his hand away. Khalid's tongue did not stop cursing the airline company and raining imprecations upon them. When we got into the aircraft we were out of breath. It was not easy for us to be taken to our seats. My brother went on damning the airline. Father kept looking first at Khalid, then at the stewardesses. His looks were gloomy and showed pain at all this din, disturbance and confusion. We finally sat down, Father by the window and Khalid next to him. Between my brother and myself sat a European passenger who seemed to be a businessman. When the steward came by with newspapers and magazines he chose *The Financial Times*. The stewardesses passed by with drinks and then explained what we should do in the event of an emergency. Use the oxygen mask and put on the life jacket and escape. Get to know the exits that would open up so that in an emergency the passengers would be able to get out.

The plane took off. They brought us some damp warm flannels. I wiped my face and neck with mine and removed the traces of sweat that had poured down when we had been waiting outside. I felt a bit more refreshed. Khalid wiped his face with his flannel but gave Father's straight back to the stewardess. I deplored what he did. Why did he not give it to Father? I wanted to say something but kept quiet. There did not seem to be any great concern on Father's face about what was going on around him. The stroke had dulled him. His movements had slowed up. He had become very forgetful. The magical spark that used to shine in his eyes had become extinguished. Those two glittering diamonds had turned into two dull pieces of glass. His eyes would no longer dart swiftly around in their sockets and he would look now at people and things quite vaguely. His loud bursts of delighted laughter were things of the past replaced now by the occasional hesitant smile. In hours, no, in a few minutes, you change from someone who is strong, vigorous, bright and happy into a spectre. Your body is absolutely weak and you move with utter feebleness. Your mental powers are shattered and your spontaneity and cheerfulness are gone for ever. There are no stages. A sudden earthquake. A swift and unexpected blow. You go from one extreme to the other without being able to adjust to this total transformation, without your family, without your dear ones, without your relations, your neighbours, your friends or your enemies being able to make provision. The stewardess caught my attention and announced with a smile, 'You can unfasten your safety belt and smoke now.'

I thanked her and explained that I did not smoke. She asked me why I had chosen to sit in the smoking section of the plane. I pointed to my brother. She nodded and went away. Khalid had lit up one cigarette for himself and another which he gave to Father. Father had given up smoking four years before his stroke. Then he took it up again, egged on by Khalid. When I spoke to him about it he said, 'What pleasures are there left to him? He can't go shopping. He's incapable of tasting appetising food. The pleasures of the night are finished. But cigarettes can relax him.'

I spoke to the doctor dealing with him. He said, 'Three or four cigarettes a day won't do him any harm. But he must take care if he smokes too much.'

When I repeated this to a doctor friend of mine he was amazed and said, 'All I know is that cigarettes do harm to those who are fit. How can they help the unfit?'

I went to the lavatory. When I returned I passed by Father's seat. I smiled and said sympathetically, 'Are you enjoying the journey?'

He said quietly, with distress in his voice, 'When . . . when . . . when will we be going back?'

I said with some surprise, 'Where to?'

He replied sadly, 'To . . . to our home . . . I . . . I'm . . . hungry . . . and feel tired.'

He was plunging a knife into my heart. These distressing words issued from a wonderful man who had been addicted to travel and to going from one place to another. When we were small he would take us on trips by land to Ras al Khaimah, Fujaira, Kalba and Khor Fukkan. He would be as merry as a child when we lit the fire outside our tent. And when we were older he took us to the cities of the east, to Bombay, Karachi, Shiraz, Cairo, Damascus and Beirut where he used to delight in haggling with the shopkeepers

145

in the suqs of those towns. He loved to sip the soft drinks sold by itinerant salesmen from vehicles or from the waterskins they carried. But now he had closed his mind to the idea of travelling. I said, trying to encourage him, 'You will eat and rest and you're going to enjoy it all, God willing.'

He did not reply. I went back to my seat, mortified by a grief that hovered over my spirits. I drank the juice I had asked for but it was without any taste. I looked towards Father. My brother had ordered a can of beer and was pouring it into a glass. Had Father been in his normal state, Khalid would never have dared do that. Father abominated strong drink and regarded with anathema people who drank. In his youth he used to drink a lot. He then gave up and always used to say on the subject, 'I lost five years of my life. The bottle held me prisoner and possessed me. I lost the pleasure of taste and the delights of women and the glory of friendship. I took no notice of the sunrise, of the light of the moon, of cold or heat, of the approach of seagulls, of the rise of prices, of new streets or buildings, of relations or my family, or of the vicissitudes in the affairs of mankind. The bottle is a curse, a curse, a curse.' Father did not look in my brother's direction. His baffled and distracted gaze was directed towards a child – who was playing with a pink toy tiger in the gangway. Khalid could have gone to the stewards' cabin to drink his can of beer. He did not drink a lot and throughout the whole journey was happy with just one or two cans. But he chose to drink sitting in his seat. Did he want to hurt Father? It could have been his usual disregard for others or his gauche timing of what he did. How do you give advice to your elder brother? You cannot. Even if you can, what is the effect of advice on a personality that is fully formed and has settled down with all its biological and psychological components?

The stewardesses brought trays of food. They placed them in front of us. Father tried to open the plastic bag containing knives, forks and spoons. His hands shook. His movements were more jerky than was necessary. The contents of the bag got scattered on the floor. Father looked at Khalid and myself sadly and apologetically. Khalid and I got up to clear up the cutlery that was all over the place. A stewardess and a passenger helped us. Khalid was muttering angrily in a low voice, 'We've become a spectacle for the other passengers. We've become a laughing stock.'

Once again he was making irresponsibly facetious comments.

Why had he not helped Father in the first place when he wanted to open the packet? The stewardess brought Father another set of implements, opened them for him and arranged them in front of him. A little while passed without him touching his food. When Khalid asked him to eat he began to eat with slow deliberation. There was less conversation in the plane and voices were lowered as the mouths of the passengers busied themselves with drinking and chewing and swallowing. I ate the salad and the cake. My dislike of mushrooms made me not touch the main course which they brought – a casserole of meat with mushrooms and rice. When I finished my meal I turned towards Father. He had eaten the main course, and gravy was dripping from his lips and beard and rice was scattered on the front of his white thawb and on his jacket. Once more the knife plunged into my heart. I wanted to draw Khalid's attention to it or to get up myself to clean up his face and clothes. I hesitated. Which was the better course of action? What would cause least embarrassment? The stewardess came and saved the situation. She came to take the tray away from Father but not before wiping the gravy from his lips and beard. She cleaned away the rice from his thawb and jacket with brisk professionalism, smiling pleasantly.

Father whispered into Khalid's ear. Khalid called me over. Father was wanting to go to the lavatory. We escorted him and stood outside, wondering whether if the door was locked behind him he would panic and be unable to open it. Then somebody went past us, coming from the first class cabin. He was an elderly European gentleman. He was without any doubt fifteen or twenty years at least older than Father. He walked with the sprightliness of a gazelle. I nudged Khalid's arm and pointed to him. He did not comprehend and I had to explain saying, 'He's older than Father.'

He said with disinterest, 'That's life.'

When we returned to our seats the lights of the aircraft were dimmed and they began to show an American film. I did not hire any ear phones for the film or for the music. I was tired and wanted to sleep. I saw the beginning of the film, which took place on a sea shore with white sands on which there were rows of coconut trees. A lot of people were bathing. A group of young men were having a race. They all had athletic bodies, supple and slender. The film focussed on a young man in the lead. He seemed to be the central character. He was shown in slow motion

147

with the strong muscles of his thighs, his slim body, his broad chest that had a coating of fair hair, his thin buttocks, his strong shoulders, his long neck, his handsome face, his blue eyes. We were also shown his rival who had an athletic body too but his face was not so beautiful. One of the girls who was watching, dressed in a suggestive bikini that hardly covered her body, shouted enthusiastic encouragement to the young man who was racing ahead. Her little breasts shook. Before he reached the winning tape the hero stumbled and fell and his rival won. The girl who was urging him on covered her face with her hands and wept. The scene moved to a hospital where the handsome fair-haired young man lay on a bed in an operating theatre. He was under an anaesthetic and the doctors looking after him were talking. The talk went on.

Travel weariness began to have its effect on my body. My eyes closed. After a little while I saw my brother Khalid playing football on the beach. I wanted him to pass the ball in my direction but he ran far away with it. I ran after him. He disappeared. I was confused and sat down watching the seagulls. They were eating blue and white jellyfish. They would tear them apart with their beaks. They would raise them up and then swallow them. I heard the sound of a drum. I could not tell where it was coming from. It was coming from all directions. A big bird passed by me. It had a child's head and said, 'Do you want to see the wedding?'

I replied 'Yes'. He told me to follow him. I ran after him and passed some large sand-dunes and then went back to the sea-shore. I saw some people gathered together. They were all men and they did not have any clothes on. Among them I noticed Father and my brother. I asked them what was going on. They told me to keep quiet and watch. The sun had begun to disappear into the sea. One of them near me lit a torch and carried it in his hand. The sea brought up a huge wooden coffin. The men went down to it and opened it up. We saw in it the dead body of my mother, her eyes closed, draped in a green shroud. Father belched but my brother began to wail and laugh. I felt the heat coming from the flaming torch near my face and moved. I woke up. My neighbour, the European businessman, had lit a huge cigar. He said apologetically, 'Is the cigar smoke troubling you?'

I replied 'No'. I looked at Father. He was asleep. Khalid was following what was going on in the film. The fair-haired young man was talking to the girl. He seemed to be asking her something, pleading with her, and so she was replying vigorously and vehemently. My eyes clouded over once more. My sleep was interrupted and not restful. I saw Father asleep on a wooden bed without any sheets or blankets. He was covered only by a white shawl, his chest was matted with white hair and his face twitched like that of an epileptic or of a man convulsed by fever. I heard Khalid say, 'Don't go near him. Leave him where he is. Don't touch him. He's ill. Run away. Scram.'

My ears were deaf to what Khalid was saying. I gently touched Father's arm. I asked him to speak to me. He opened his eyes wearily. When he opened his mouth a rattle-like noise came out and blood trickled from his lips. I woke up in panic. Everybody was asleep, the film was over and the small child was still playing with his pink toy tiger, making its head turn and moving its legs.

I went to the lavatory and washed my face. I looked at my eyes in the mirror. They were deep red. I cursed sleeping on aeroplanes. It is exhausting and unsettling. As we approached London, there was a stir of activity among both passengers and cabin staff. More people were going to the lavatory. The stewardesses were serving tea, coffee, water, fresh drinks and alcohol. The iqal and ghutra on Father's head had got lopsided. Khalid tried to adjust it as it had been before. Father took on the appearance of Europeans who wore the iqal and ghutra. It was wrong, unbalanced, uncoordinated and unnatural.

The stewardess came and fastened Father's safety belt. When the plane had landed at Heathrow airport we had no difficulty getting Father to the wheel-chair because the aeroplane door gave directly on to an airport corridor. We walked along the long corridor. After we completed the immigration formalities we made our way to the baggage collection hall. My suitcase arrived and so did Father's but Khalid's did not. We waited a long time. The suitcase did not turn up. Khalid got more and more angry. He damned the airline and the English airport officials and said, 'The airline is lousy and these English are finished. They'll soon be at the bottom of the league of European states. They're finished. Done for.'

We went to the office dealing with lost and missing baggage. They gave us a form and took our London address. Outside the London weather was rainy and a grey foggy atmosphere touched

149

everything. We put our two suitcases into a big black taxi. But we had great difficulty trying to get Father inside. His joints were uncoordinated. He gripped the wheel-chair firmly. Khalid shouted at him, 'Let go of the wheel-chair. We'll help you. Let go of the wheel-chair.'

He let go of the wheel-chair but had problems getting right into the taxi. There was no balance in his movements. His iqal fell to the ground and got wet and muddy. I picked it up and gave it back to him. Anxiety and distress showed on his face. We were at last able to get him in. The taxi set off. Khalid told him angrily, 'Oooh, you've hurt us and embarrassed us. You clung on to the door quite unnecessarily. You made people laugh at us. You're a disaster. Your iqal fell off and got filthy. You're a complete disaster.'

Father looked into Khalid's angry face and stuttered sadly and helplessly, 'I . . . can . . . not . . .I . . . don't . . . know . . . it's out . . . of my hands . . . I'm . . . tired . . . take me . . . home.'

At that I could no longer contain myself and snapped at Khalid, 'You're despicable . . . you're thick . . . you're a fool . . . you're a stupid idiot. Have you lost all sense of love and duty and respect, that you speak to him like that? . . . Couldn't you see the look of pain, confusion, alarm and humiliation in his eyes when his cutlery went all over the place, when he was outside the toilet and when he was sitting in a wheel-chair in the middle of hundreds of strong healthy people able to walk around . . . you're despicable . . . you're totally insensitive.'

I was unable to go on. My face became flushed. I was choking with distress and burst into tears.

Geographical Note

The emirate of Dubai is on the Gulf and faces north west. It is one of seven emirates that make up the United Arab Emirates. The capital is Abu Dhabi, 160 kilometres on the coast to the south west. Sharjah, Ajman, Umm al Quwain and Ras al Khaimah are emirates on the Gulf coast to the north. Facing the Indian ocean is the emirate of Fujaira. Khor Fukkan and Dibba are towns also on the Indian ocean coast. The Arabian landmass tapers to a peninsula, Ruus al Jibal, which is Omani territory.

The city of Dubai bestrides a creek. The old quarters on the south side are Shindagha and Ber Dubai. The northern side of the creek is known generally as Deira. Murshid suq and Sanadiq suq are older commercial areas on the Deira side of the city.

Dhaid is an oasis town outside the emirate on the road to the Indian ocean coast. Khawanij and al Awir are oasis villages within twenty miles of Dubai. Jabal Ali is on the road to Abu Dhabi. Linja is an island off the coast of Iran which has long had commercial and cultural links with Dubai.

Rashidiya and Qusais are inland newly developed suburbs to the north east. Manama and Hamriya are suburbs to the north of the creek near the coast. Jafiliya and Satwa are suburbs south of the creek and inland from Jumaira which is on the coast.

Glossary

aba'a: black cloak worn by women.

Abdul Halim: Abdul Halim Hafez, Egyptian singer.

Abdul Wahhab: Muhammad Abdul Wahhab, doyen of Egyptian singers.

abu: father. Abu Ahmad, the name given to somebody who is the father of Ahmad.

Ali al Rawgha: singer from Abu Dhabi.

al Kindi: 9th century Arab philosopher of Baghdad.

bisht: men's cloak.

burqu': mask over the eyes and nose, worn as a veil by women.

dirham: UAE unit of currency. In 1990 equal to 16p.

dishdasha: white smock worn by men.

falafil: spicy, deep-fried croquettes.

faluda: Indian sweetmeat.

Fuhaihil: town to south of Kuwait city.

ghutra: headcloth, often checkered, worn by men.

harisa: common meat dish.

humus: paste made from chickpeas.

Ibn al Maqaffa: 8th century Arab writer.

imam: leader of prayers, official attached to a mosque.

iqal: the cord that circles the headcloth.

Ismail Yasin: Egyptian comic actor.

Jahiliya: the period before Islam.

Jahiz: 9th century writer of Iraq.

jallabiya: smock worn by men and women.

lawz: tree resembling the almond.

Mahdawi: Iraqi army officer who presided over the Revolutionary court after the 1958 Revolution.

Mahmoud Darwish: contemporary Palestinian poet.

majlis: sitting room, session.

Manfaluti: 20th century Egyptian writer.

mazza: variety of salad dishes.

muezzin: the man who calls people to prayer.

Muhammad Abdu: Sa'udi singer.

Muhid Hamad: singer from Umm al Quwain.

Mutanabbi: 10th century Arab poet.

Nabati: popular demotic poetry of the Arabian penins.lar.

Naguib Mahfouz: Egyptian novelist, Nobel prize winner 1988.

Nizar Qabbani: contemporary Syrian poet.

Qais and Laila: idealised lovers of classical Arab tradition.

Rabab: Kuwaiti singer.

Riyal: Sau'di Arabian unit of currency. (In 1990 equal to 14p.)

ruq'a: a cursive style of calligraphy.

sambusa: crescent shaped pastry sandwich with meat or cheese.

sayyid: holy man, popularly believed to be a descendant of the
Prophet Muhammad.

shawarma: charcoal-broiled mutton, cut in thin slices from a joint
on a vertical skewer.

Shawqi: early 20th century Egyptian poet.

sidr: lotus tree.

Suad Muhammad: Arab woman singer.

suq: market, shopping centre.

taqia: skull cap.

thawb: dress, used for men and women.

umm: mother; Umm Khalid, name given to a woman who is the mother
of Khalid.

Umm Kulthum: most celebrated of modern Arab singers, Egyptian,
died 1973.

Warda: Egyptian woman singer.

Yusuf Idris: contemporary Egyptian novelist.